SWIMMING DEAD

VICTORIA MATTSEN CRIME SERIES
BOOK 2

IFEANYI ESIMAI

ShotReads

eISBN: 978-1-63589-784-5

Print ISBN: 978-1-63589-785-2

Hardcover ISBN: 978-1-63589-786-9

Get a FREE copy of The Rookie!

Join my Newsletter for updates, giveaways, teasers, and a FREE copy of the prequel - The Rookie. Click here or scan the QR code.

For Chinwe...Always.
The wind beneath my wings.

ACKNOWLEDGMENTS

My heartfelt gratitude goes out to my family and friends, whose unwavering faith in me fueled this project from the very start.

I also want to extend a special thanks to a group of incredible individuals whose generous spirit has made an indelible impact on this project, and for that, I am forever grateful.

Erik S
Nneka Anaebonam
Craig Martelle
Jenn Davidson
Chinwe Anyamele
Obioha Emezie
Renee
Okechukwu Obua
Romeo Richards
Ikenna Emeghara
Charles Onunkwo
Adaeze

Every one of you has helped shape this journey in your own unique way, and I couldn't be more thankful. Your support has not only made these books a reality but has also inspired me as I continue to tell Detective Vikki Mattsen's story.

To all the readers, thank you for inviting Detective Vikki

Mattsen into your lives. It's been a joy to share this adventure with you.

Here's to the stories yet to be told.

PROLOGUE

She was all over him like a vulture circling a dying animal—something was up, but he couldn't put a finger on it.

"I'll shower, then we'll do it," she said. Her voice was a sexy purr. She shed the last of her clothing and headed for the bathroom.

He didn't want to look, but it had a magnetic attraction. Her jet-black hair fell to the middle of her back against golden tanned skin. Her legs went on forever. His eyes were glued to her heart-shaped ass—the eighth wonder of the world.

She disappeared into the bathroom. The shower came on, and she sang. Maybe this was his opportunity to bail. The room swayed. His head throbbed, signaling the beginning of a headache. Was it the vodka? It'd tasted a little different—some strong Russian shit. He shook his head. The room stopped moving.

He didn't want to 'do it.' How should he remove himself? Feign tiredness? Or say he had some disease?

The thought of a disease and his penis falling off made his balls retreat, mirroring a turtle's withdrawal into its shell.

Good.

Now, which disease should he tell her? HIV? Syphilis? Gonorrhea? Maybe ticks. He had a sudden breakthrough— COVID! Dick Covid. That could be a movie star's name. He was lost in his thoughts when the bathroom door burst open. She sauntered in—wet, naked, and ready.

She was a leopard about to pounce on its prey. "I love your dreamy eyes."

He saw an opening—to say he was tired. "I don't think—"

She threw her arms around his neck. The smell of wild-flowers and vanilla filled his nostrils.

She leaned close to his ear and said, "Sweetheart, I need you right now." Her voice was a whisper. Her breath, pure heat against his skin. She nibbled on his earlobe, then traced a wet path down his neck.

All the self-affirmation he'd given himself minutes earlier flew out of the window. There was no escape. He was a man, after all. He went from zero to steel in milliseconds.

Maybe, just this once.

Her fingers did a quick work of his belt and zipper. His jeans fell, bunched up around his ankles.

"God." The word shuddered out of him.

She shoved him, and he fell onto the bed. She crawled on top of him, kissing his forehead, cheeks, and lips. She guided him inside her, enveloping him with her warmth.

He moaned. They were off to the races.

She rose and fell at a furious pace—no doubt who was in control. Her lovemaking was always on steroids as she chased another release.

After she finished with him, he felt as if he'd survived eight rounds with Mike Tyson in the ring.

"Now, let's go and relax in the hot tub." She helped him up.

It didn't look like sleep was on her agenda. He didn't want

to move but didn't want to make her suspicious. The sex was good, but there was a type of clarity one attains after an orgasm. He must get away from her before it was too late.

She opened the sliding door, and he stumbled along.

The warm air outside felt good on his naked skin. He looked up and took a deep breath. The night sky was full of stars. The blinking light of a plane cut across the sky.

She led him to the tub. "Ah, always ready for me. Now sit. Don't go anywhere. I'll be right back."

He climbed on. The tub wobbled, and he held the sides for support. He'd spend the night. In the morning, he'd be out of here for good. He could not be a part of this.

"Ah." He let out a sigh. The water was warm. The sprays and jets were soothing and caressing. A worthwhile alternative to a Masseuse. He felt sleepy. The sound of splashing waves generated in the tub didn't help—a lullaby. He blinked repeatedly, trying to keep his eyes open.

"Here you go." She handed him a wine glass filled to the brim with a clear liquid. She sat next to him. "Cheers."

He lifted his glass and sniffed—more vodka. "Thank you." He took a sip. It tasted like the last one—bitter. Scared he might drop it, he downed it in one gulp and placed the empty glass on the edge of the tub. He relaxed, both arms stretched out on the side of the tub.

She traced circles on his chest and nibbled his ear. "Have I told you today how wonderful you make me feel?" Her voice was sexy and seductive. "You are a miracle worker."

His eyes fluttered. He needed a miracle to keep them open. "You are the miracle worker," he said. But no words came out. It was all in his head. His vision became foggy. He slid down the tub.

She giggled. "What are you doing?"

The water climbed up his face—chin, mouth, nose. He held his breath. The water stung his eyes. He tried to raise his head. His body refused to obey him. His heart raced. He had the sensation of being smothered. Yet, his body refused to move.

Water went over his head, a gurgling sound bubbling in his ears. He needed air.

That was his last conscious thought.

CHAPTER ONE

Vikki sprang off the bed with a suddenness reminiscent of a Jack-in-the-box. The bed springs groaned.

"Where are you going?" Ted said.

"Time to go." She picked up her panties, bra, jeans, and t-shirt and headed for the bathroom. She tinkled and dressed quickly. She'd take a bath when she got to her place.

"I have to go. It was a pleasure knowing you."

He opened his mouth, he hesitated. "Don't you want to know where I'm going? How to get in touch?"

"Not in the least. It's better this way. It was fun while it lasted." She headed for the door. Knowing she was lying to herself brought on anger. Something was brewing in her heart, too. Maybe a woman's heart was not where everyone believed it was.

"Vikki!"

She turned. "What?"

Their eyes met.

It was her turn to mimic a hands-off gesture. "Sorry, I didn't mean to sound like that."

"Did someone hurt you deeply in the past?" His voice was

soft and low. "I'm a good listener. Sharing can be therapeutic."

The silence lingered for a moment. She could tell him about Bruce—how they'd met and fallen in love. How he'd been her field training officer when she was a rookie. How she'd caused his death the day he was going to propose to her. Instead, she went on the offensive.

"Now you're my therapist?" She exhaled. "There's nothing to share, Doctor. And remember, it's not ethical for a physician to screw his patient."

He chuckled. "But you're not my—"

"Have a good morning and a safe trip." She left.

Vikki walked to her car, shielding her eyes from the sun. She was running from commitment. But there was nothing to commit to. He was leaving. Her mind drifted to the people she had called family, Alexis and her dad. It had been more than a decade since they'd been taken from her. The people behind their murder must have dropped their guards by now. She would have to start making plans. They must pay.

Vikki mounted her cell phone on the dash stand and checked her messages. Gomez had called a few times while she was with Ted. She planned to return his call later.

Gomez was her partner and planned to retire in two years to travel the world with his wife. Maybe he was calling because of a case.

She put the car in drive and headed for her home.

Vikki's home was a three-bedroom apartment on Mill Road. Once there, she made coffee, brushed her teeth, and showered. Her cell phone rang—she answered without looking to see who it was.

"Mattsen."

It was Jody, the police department's administration secretary. They exchanged pleasantries.

Jody was sixty-five and widowed. SIPD and her cats were

all the family she needed to keep her going. She'd been there longer than everyone else and knew everything. She was the person to talk to if you had questions about the police department or needed favors.

"Vikki, there's a floater on Lake St. Ives. The captain wants you to lead."

"I'll be there."

CHAPTER TWO

Vikki drove past old farms with red barns and grazing livestock. Picture-perfect views in total contrast to the ugliness at her destination. Views like this made her think of the past and the future.

More than ten years ago, her best friend and her father had been murdered in cold blood. How far was she going to go to avenge them?

She recited her tweaked version of the law enforcement oath of honor:

I will always have the courage to hold others accountable for their actions.

Vikki smiled. An eye for an eye. Here she was, a detective who had sworn under oath to serve and protect, thinking about committing murder. Thoughts become things.

The sun shimmered off the surface of the lake as she approached. She drove toward two parked police cruisers with flashing lights. A few onlookers watched from a distance, far from the yellow police tape. Good. She'd talk to them later.

Next to the cruisers was the ME's van. Vikki was

surprised Gomez's car wasn't there. Maybe he drove up in one of the cruisers.

Vikki stepped out of her car to the earthy smell of the lake and headed toward the cordoned-off area with a uniform standing guard. The heels of her shoes sank into the soft sand. She looked at the rest of her clothing: tan-colored pants, a white blouse, and a light cream jacket to cover her Glock. She hoped she wasn't overdressed.

"Good morning, detective," the uniform said. He held open the crime logbook.

Vikki picked up the pen in the middle—printed and signed her name. She recognized one of the names already on the log.

"Thanks." She took the CSO he held up for her.

She dressed quickly in the crime scene overall, covered her shoes, and slipped under the yellow tape. The victim, a naked Caucasian male, lay on a stretcher in a body bag zipped up to the waist. A crime scene technician in CSO was on his knees over the body.

Two officers in scuba diving suits stood a few feet from the body. Vikki recognized Vinny Russo.

"Hi, Vinny." Vikki nodded at the other officer, whose name skipped her mind.

Russo was in his late twenties and had been with the SIPD longer than Vikki. He and the other officer make up the department's underwater recovery unit. They split their time between patrols and body recovery. She believed this was their first or second recovery since their training.

Vinny smiled. "Victoria, how are you?"

He was one of the few people who called her Victoria—he said it was his late mother's name. Why were they in diving outfits? "Wasn't the victim floating?"

Vinny shook his head. "No. The lungs fill with water and weigh the body down at the bottom. But eventually, it rises like a buoy, forced up by released gases as decomposition sets in."

Vikki nodded. Jody must have used the word floater loosely. She wondered how the body was discovered if it was submerged. She waited for him to get to it.

"In frigid water, decomposition might not be rapid, and the body never surfaces." Vinny shrugged. "Sometimes, it gets entangled in a plant, fishing net, or what have you at the bottom."

Vinny had clear plastic containers in each hand that looked like infusion bags—normal saline or dextrose. But the liquid in them was brownish. "What are those?" Vikki asked.

Vinny hefted them in his palms. "Whirl-pak bags containing lake water. We collected water samples around the body. Hopefully, they'll come in handy for the ME in determining the cause and manner of death.

Vikki nodded. "Do you know who found him?"

Vinny tipped his head to his right. "The couple over there. He was proposing to her last night, and the ring fell into the drink. They decided to dive down this morning and look for it. They got more than they bargained for. They found him about two hours ago."

A man and woman, probably in their early twenties, sat together with towels over their shoulders. A uniform with a notepad stood in front of them, talking and occasionally taking notes.

Vikki couldn't imagine what was going through the minds of the couple. Their first step to a new life together had degenerated into a nightmare.

"Any ID on the victim? Anything to identify him by?"

Vinny shook his head. "He was in his birthday suit. I can't say if he started swimming like that or his trunks got snagged on something. It might surface later if he had a pair and they came off."

A multitude of questions crossed Vikki's mind. Was his death a misadventure? Suicide? She glanced around again, wondering where Dr. Patel was. What was the time of death? She must talk to the CSU tech for the latter.

The uniform with the couple folded his pad and walked toward the cruisers.

Vikki jumped on the opportunity. "Thanks, Vinny. I'll go talk to the couple."

She checked them out as she approached. The guy was skinny—looked like an inverted pyramid—a swimmer's body. The girl was petite—had the body of a gymnast. Both had black hair and matching costumes. Black trunks for the guy and a one-piece black swimsuit for the girl. Did they have anything to do with this?

"Hello, I'm Detective Vikki Mattsen. I'm sorry for what happened to your friend."

The girl went bug-eyed. "He's not our friend. We met him for the first time underwater...this morning."

"Never seen him before," said the man. He exhaled. "We went looking for a ring I dropped in the water last night while proposing."

Vikki brought out a notepad and pen from her coat pocket. "I hope you don't mind; I'm going to ask both of you a few questions about what happened."

The man's name was Zac Callahan, and the woman was Lisa Monroe. Both had graduated from Rutgers and lived in the next town.

"We've already talked to the officer," said Zac, in a flat monotone. "I'd been saving for that ring, and it fell into the lake."

Lisa rubbed his shoulder. "It's okay, babe. We have each other."

They reiterated what Officer Russo had said. Vikki reminded herself to read the officer's report back at the PD.

"Did you see anything suspicious last night or this morning?"

"If there were, I didn't notice," Zac said. "I was anxious about what to say to her."

Lisa pursed her lips. "Same here. He'd hinted about how he'd propose. When we got to the lake, and he said we should row out, I kind of knew. I was focused on the moment."

Vikki nodded. "So, you rowed out. Do you know what time that was?"

"I'll say around eight," said Lisa.

Vikki wrote on her pad. "What happened next?"

"Zac stopped rowing and got on one knee. The canoe rocked, then steadied. Zac brought out the ring. He took my hand...proposed, and I said yes. Then when he was about to slip the ring on my finger, the boat wobbled." A sob escaped Lisa's throat. "He lost his balance. The ring sailed out of his hand and into the lake."

"Did anybody see what happened?"

"I don't know, but there were people here," Lisa said, pointing to the shore. "It was a full moon."

Zac's shoulders sagged. "People were having dinner at the restaurant, and music from there was fading in and out. I don't know if they noticed."

"Excuse me, Detective Mattsen?" said a voice.

Vikki glanced in the direction the voice had come from. It was the CSU technician. His eyes sparkled like a kid who'd just discovered that the word 'read' was spelled the same, present or past tense.

"You have to come and see this."

Vikki's pulse picked up a notch. What was it? She brought out her business card and handed it to Lisa. "If you guys remember anything, call me." She turned to walk away.

"Can we leave?" Zac asked, one eyebrow raised.

Vikki stopped—glanced at the police officer, then back to them. "Sure, we'll call if we need more information."

Zac let out a huge breath.

Lisa mumbled and said, "Thank you, God."

Vikki walked over to the technician. "What do you have?"

CHAPTER THREE

The CSU technician held up both of the victim's hands.

The skin pads of each of the fingers and the thumbs appeared to have been nibbled. Like an open wound—yellowish and pink. Was someone trying to hide something? or did the wildlife stumble upon an unexpected feast?

Vikki swallowed. Her lips curled. "Did fish do that?"

The tech shook his head. "I can't say for sure."

"How long do you think he's been in the water?"

Beads of sweat dotted his forehead. "Dr. Patel will be in a better position to answer that. I'll say about twenty-four to forty-eight hours."

"Where is Dr. Patel anyway? Even Gomez is not here."

The technician chuckled. "Sorry, I don't know. I'm beginning to sound like a broken record."

"All right, thanks," said Vikki.

The technician went back to examining the victim.

Vikki glanced at the few houses not far from them. They all had similar designs with minor differences in color and finishing—single-story buildings from the street, two at the back with a commanding view of the lake.

Vikki headed to the nearest house. There was no bell. She knocked, waited a few seconds then banged on the door with the heel of her palm. Nobody came. The next one was the same. She went to the third one. Thank God there was a bell. She pressed it. A cat sat on the window ledge, staring out. A dog barked somewhere in the house.

Vikki was about to leave when the echo of approaching footsteps reached her. A woman's face appeared in the window. Vikki smiled, raised her badge, and mouthed, "Police."

The face disappeared. Seconds later, the door opened.

A poodle mix ran out, danced around Vikki's legs, then collapsed on the ground, kicking its feet in the air.

Vikki bent down. Laughing, she said, "Cute doggy." She gave it belly rubs. The dog got back on its feet and bolted back into the house. Vikki straightened up.

"How can I help you."

Vikki almost jerked back. Her voice was loud. She was probably in her late sixties. Her hair was all gray and went with the flower pattern sundress. She smelled of bathing soap.

"Good morning. Sorry to bother you. I'm Detective Mattsen with SIPD. We're—"

"What!" She cupped her ear.

"I'm Detective Mattsen!"

She nodded and fanned herself. "It's hot. That's why I have this sundress on!"

Vikki had her badge up again. She pressed on, this time slowly, picking her words. "We recovered a dead body from the lake. Did you hear or see anything last night?"

Another lady came to the door and said, "Sorry, Detective, my mother must have forgotten to put on her hearing aid. I'm Laura May." She glanced at her mother and tapped a finger against her.

The older lady touched her ear. "Darn. I'll be right back!"

"I saw police activity through the window," said Laura May. "Did someone drown?"

Vikki nodded. "Yes, I was wondering if you heard or saw anything last night?"

Laura sighed. "Oh, poor soul. I hope it wasn't a child." She shook her head. "People are always coming and going, especially now that the weather is much warmer. We've lived here for thirty years and have learned to block out the noise. Now and then, someone drowns. To answer your question, nothing out of the ordinary."

The mother reappeared. She touched her ear. "That's a lot better. Last night while I was watching *Family Feud*, it was making a chugging sound. What's your name again?"

Vikki extended her hand. "Detective Mattsen."

"I'm the real Laura May," said the Real Laura May, shaking Vikki's hand. "It was a pleasure meeting you. I have an episode of *Family Feud* to catch up on. Goodbye, Detective." She went back in.

"She's so sweet," Vikki said. "Do you have any security cameras?"

"Sorry, no."

Vikki pointed at the next two houses. "What about your neighbors?"

"The Allen's, first house, Robbins second house. The two families went on vacation together. They've been gone for about a week. Another week to go. I don't think they have cameras, either. It's relatively safe around here." She sighed. "The problem we have, especially in the summer, is people letting it all *hang out*—indecent exposure."

Vikki gave Laura May her card. "Thanks so much for your time. If you remember anything, please reach out."

"I will." Laura May bit her lower lip as if in thought. Then she said, "I think I've seen cameras at Lakefront Restaurant. You should try them."

"Thanks for your time." Vikki headed to the restaurant. A beautiful long white building with gardens designed to complement the lake. She scanned the junction between the wall and roof corners where she expected to see cameras and saw one. She let out a sigh of relief. "All right, maybe we can get to the bottom of this."

To her right was the lake. The yellow tape was still there, and only one cruiser remained. The victim must have been loaded onto the ME's van. She made a mental note to visit the ME once she got back to the PD.

Vikki climbed up the stairs to the entrance. She opened the door to the reception committee—the smell of bacon, coffee, and pastries. Her stomach rumbled. A woman in her early twenties was behind the counter. Her shirt and pants were black. Her blonde hair was pulled in a ponytail.

She gave Vikki a cheerful smile. "Table for one?"

Vikki explained who she was, why she was there, and what she wanted. The girl's face turned the color of yogurt when she heard someone had drowned last night.

"Oh my God. I'll get the manager."

Vikki surveyed her surroundings. Framed black-and-white photos of local high school sports teams and people she didn't recognize hung on the walls. One wall was all glass, showing a magnificent clear view of the lake. It must be amazing at night, with lights shimmering off the lake's surface.

"Detective Mattsen?" said a male voice behind her.

Vikki turned. A man—the manager with a salt-and-pepper goatee, approached. His eyes widened. Vikki knew why.

"Oh, I didn't..." He caught himself.

He didn't expect a woman Vikki wanted to finish for him.

"I'm Paul Zel, the owner. I heard—someone drowned here last night."

"I'm afraid so," Vikki said. "Mr. Zel, we need your help."

"Please call me Paul."

Vikki didn't return the favor. Detective Mattsen was okay with her. "Paul, I noticed the security cameras. Can I see the videos, especially the ones covering the lake, if you don't mind?"

"Sure, no problem, this way."

He walked through the quiet bar to the back, and Vikki followed. He stopped at the door with Staff Only written on it in bold text.

"I'd also like to talk to your staff that was here last night."

Paul rested his hand on the doorknob. "You'll have to come back at night to see them."

CHAPTER FOUR

Vikki returned to the PD. In her pocket was a thumb drive with the video recording from Lakefront Restaurant. Where was Gomez? She'd called him twice on her drive back, and it had gone straight to voice mail.

She stopped at Jody's desk. "Hi, Jody. I've been trying to reach Gomez. He wasn't at the crime scene. Did he call in?"

Jody raised an eyebrow. "You haven't heard?"

Vikki's stomach lurched, feeling as though it had suddenly catapulted into her throat. "N-no. Heard...heard what?" She stilled herself. She hadn't known she cared so much for her partner of two years.

Jody looked around, leaned in conspiratorially, and whispered, "His buddy, Dr. Patel—you notice he's been losing weight."

Vikki nodded.

"I heard he has pancreatic cancer and wants to visit the country of his birth one more time. He asked Gomez to take him to the airport. He's keeping it to himself."

"He should have—" Vikki stopped. You respected people's privacy. "I'm so sorry to hear that. No wonder Dr. Patel wasn't at the crime scene," she whispered back. Her thoughts drifted to Bruce Bruckner, Alexis, and Michael Devoe. People she'd lost without warning. It was never easy. "Thanks."

Vikki headed to the detective squad room. Gomez should have told her. Didn't he trust her? Now they had a medical examiner issue, too. She passed Gomez's table and threw herself into her chair.

"Detective Mattsen," said a deep, scratchy voice.

Vikki rolled her eyes. She knew who it was. When was this going to stop? She and McClane had been at 64th precinct in Brooklyn back in the day when she was a rookie. He touched her at The Bull Dog bar, and she'd defended herself.

McClane ended up in a hospital, and now he jumped at every opportunity to make her look bad. One of these days, she would take matters into her own hands.

"Hey, Runway! With your partner gone, I can guess how many cases you'll be able to close. None!" He roared with laughter.

Because she'd done some modeling while in college in Paris, some of her friends from the police academy called her that.

Vikki shook her head and concentrated on what to do next. She needed a sketch of the victim's face, then watch the video from the restaurant. Mr. Zel was kind enough to make her a copy. In the background, McClane, the dickhead, continued to talk loud and crack jokes at her expense.

This was harassment. Vikki's hand drifted toward her Glock. That should shut him up for good. That wasn't an option. The best way would be to file a report. But Vikki had no intentions of filing a report against a fellow detective with Internal Affairs.

Even though McClane had no audience per se, he continued.

His voice boomed. "I remember...I remember—"

Suddenly, his voice died down like a switch had been turned off. Vikki looked up, hoping McClane had bitten his tongue off and was choking on it. Instead, Mike Gomez walked in, his facial expression turned down. Dressed in a black suit, black shirt, and tie, he could've been coming from a funeral.

Gomez took off his jacket, hung it on his chair, and sat. He turned to Vikki and attempted a smile. "You want me to talk to the captain about him?" He jerked his head toward McClane.

"No, I'll take care of it my way," Vikki said. "Don't worry about it."

Gomez raised his hand. "Okay. It upsets me when he runs his mouth." He took a breath and let it out through his lips. "*Really* sorry, you must have heard by now."

Vikki nodded.

"I was with Amitab all morning. I'd turned off my phone. I knew you'd call and ask questions. I wouldn't have been able to answer in front of him. He didn't want anyone to know... while he was still around. He doesn't want pity."

"I understand," Vikki said and turned away. Just last week, he was at the Appleton cabin investigating the explosion. "How does he feel?"

Gomez tried to speak, but his lips only quivered. The words refused to come. He shrugged, picked up a bunch of folders on his desk, and tapped the edges on the table to make them uniform. He was buying time, waiting for the emotions to pass.

Vikki placed a hand on his shoulder and squeezed. Words eluded her, too. She'd read somewhere that seventy-one percent of people diagnosed with pancreatic cancer had a life expectancy of less than one year.

Gomez dropped the folder back on the table and cleared his throat. "Okay, what do we have?"

She told him about the drowning. "I was thinking of how to get a forensic artist for a sketch, then watch the CCTV videos from the restaurant."

"I thought it was drowning. You think there was foul play?"

"I don't know. The fingertip injuries might have been before death. But—"

"There are no coincidences," Gomez said, finishing off for her. He took out his cell phone. "I know the artist Amitab uses. I'll call him."

While Gomez was on the phone, Vikki plugged the USB drive into her computer. The couple had lost their ring on Sunday night. Had the vic drowned on Sunday night or earlier? She took a gamble. She forwarded the time-stamped video to Saturday night and clicked 'play.'

The camera was focused on the restaurant's door. It captured a little of the lake and people going in and leaving the restaurant.

"Done." Gomez lowered his phone. "He'll be here within the hour, and we'll have our sketch." He leaned closer. "Is that the restaurant?"

"Yeah."

"Wait a minute. I've been there for lunch...with my wife. They serve amazing lasagna."

"Mattsen! Gomez!"

They both looked up in the direction the voice had come from. Captain Levin stood by the door to his office, his face stern. He waved them over.

CHAPTER FIVE

Captain Levin shut the office door. He walked over to the other side of his executive table and sat. He ran his hand over his navy-blue suit. Today, his red tie against a blue shirt. Behind him on the wall were two portraits, one of him and the other of the mayor. He gestured at the two chairs on the other side. "Sit."

Vikki hoped for a short meeting. She had nothing yet on the case.

"So, Dr. Patel is off to India?" Captain Levin said. "Was that the best decision?"

Gomez shrugged. "That's what he wanted."

Levin nodded. "I hope everything works out the way he planned."

"I hope so, too."

The captain formed a teepee with his fingers. "Mattsen, you were at the lake. What do we have?"

"Caucasian male, mid-to-late twenties. Found by a couple who dove into the lake to recover an engagement ring they'd dropped on Sunday night. So far, nobody saw or heard anything. A forensic artist is coming to create a sketch. We can try to ID him. I was about to review some CCTV footage from a nearby restaurant."

Levin frowned. "Fingers compromised?"

"Yes, sir. The tips of all eight fingers and two thumbs were either feasted on by hungry lake inhabitants or deliberately disfigured."

Gomez turned to Vikki. "Possible homicide?"

"We'll know in due course," Vikki said.

The captain inhaled and let it out in a rush through his nose. He leaned forward. "I spoke with the mayor, and he wants us to get to the bottom of this as soon as possible. With summer almost upon us, he doesn't want a drawn-out investigation. It will hurt the town's coffers if people think the lake is not safe and go somewhere else to vacation."

Vikki didn't know how to say what she wanted, but it must be said. "Without an ME at hand...things might take a little longer. Especially if it's a suspected homicide."

The chief nodded. "Yes, I discussed that with the mayor, too. We'll have an expert on loan from Sussex County Hospital as early as this afternoon. Hopefully, we'll find a temporary forensic pathologist sooner than later."

"I hope so, too," Gomez said in a low voice.

Levin clapped his hands loudly and rubbed them together. "Okay, that's about it. Keep me updated."

Back at her table, Vikki went back to the recorded video feed. "I hope we'll find something we can use."

Gomez, still standing, said, "It's been a busy morning. I'm going to the break room. You want some mud?"

Vikki made a face. The break room coffee wasn't the best. "Sure." She increased the playback speed. It was fascinating watching the clouds move faster, blotting out the sun.

There wasn't much going on. The occasional bird swooped down to grab a snack from the lake's surface. A lone canoe with one occupant rowed furiously past. Other traffic was from people walking along the shore, taking pictures with their phones.

Vikki was bored and lost in the monotony when a commotion at the other end of the office drew her attention.

"You're nothing but a little cunt," said a woman. She slurred her words and spoke with an Eastern European accent.

Vikki checked her out. A tall blonde in a tight miniskirt, revealing blouse, and stilettos. Her hands were handcuffed behind her. Escort?

Maria Santiago, the rookie detective, placed a hand on her back to direct her. She shrugged it off.

The handcuffed blonde, unsteady on her feet, said, "She was with me last night. Look at her now. All prim and proper. You should see her handle a man."

CHAPTER SIX

"Wow, wow," said Gomez, cautiously trying to squeeze past the two women while holding up two Styrofoam cups of steaming coffee. "Is that true, Detective Santiago?"

Maria turned red. "Don't mind her. She's had a little too much to drink. She'll sleep it off in a cell like yesterday."

"Yes," said the drunk blonde. "Put me in a cell. I need my beauty sleep. I want to look like Marilyn Monroe when I wake up. Last night I saw her bobbing up and down on the water."

Gomez made it back to his desk, laughing. "I thought the coffee might end up on my shirt. Did you see Maria? I've never seen anyone turn into a tomato in my life." He handed one cup to Vikki.

"What took you so long?" Vikki said. "You had to bring the coffee beans yourself?"

"Hey, watch your mouth, or I'll bring Maria's friend over here to reveal your secrets."

Vikki laughed. "I was dozing off. That little excitement woke me."

"I got held up. I saw the artist with Jody, so I gave him

directions to the morgue. He said he'll get us a composite we can use in about thirty minutes."

"Sound's great." Vikki raised her cup. "Good mud today."

Gomez nodded toward her screen. "Anything yet?"

"Nothing yet.. Hopefully, with a sketch, we'll have more options."

Gomez turned on his computer. "I have a report to type." He sighed. "No matter how small your case is, you have to write a thesis. At least it's better than when we used typewriters, then searched for the captain to read it and sign off."

They worked in silence until one of the detectives yelled out Gomez's name. Vikki raised her head. A guy walked toward them, holding a sketchbook. She nudged Gomez. "I think the artist is here."

Gomez introduced the artist to Vikki. His name was Tony, and he'd been sketching dead people for five years.

Gomez got up from his chair. "Please sit."

Tony sat. "The victim was submerged, right?"

"Yes," Vikki said. But she wanted to learn more. "How did you know?"

"The washerwoman appearance of his hands." He placed the sketchbook on the table and flipped through it. "He's been there at least five hours—up to forty-eight." He stopped at a page. "Here's my rendering."

Vikki couldn't draw to save her life, but she appreciated and marveled at how he'd caught all the little details. He produced a drawing of the vic with his eyes open.

Tony stood. "I'll see myself out. If you have any questions —you have my number."

"Won't you stay for lunch?" Gomez said.

"I'll take a rain check. Maybe by then, Patel will be back."

Vikki stood, too. "Thank you."

"But don't forget to send your bill to SIPD," Gomez said.

Vikki snapped a picture of the image with her phone. "I'll

print a few hard copies." She went over to the printer and returned with a few copies. She gave him one.

Gomez studied it. "What should we do?"

"Do you want to show the picture at the lake and restaurant? Hopefully, someone might recognize him. Or you might pick up things that I'd missed."

"It's like you read my mind," Gomez said.

"I'll check with missing persons. Once we get a name, we can notify his next of kin."

"Fine with me. See you later." Gomez left.

An hour later, Vikki went to the break room and got a Snickers bar from the vending machine and more coffee. The video had yielded nothing.

Vikki shivered as she swallowed the dredges of her coffee. It was cold and bitter. She picked up the phone. Time to call the Call-Taker Station, but then she changed her mind. That was for the public. She went downstairs to see Jody.

"You want missing person's reports for the last two days?" Jody asked.

"Yes."

Jody tapped away on the keypad as if it were an extension of her fingers. "Saturday, a five-year-old boy was reported missing at the grocery store. Found an hour later. Hmm, a woman called on Saturday at five-thirty p.m. to report her partner was missing. She last saw him on Friday."

"What's the missing person's name?" Vikki asked, her heartbeat picking up a notch. "We can run that through DMV and put a face on it."

"She never gave one. At that point, she said, 'Never mind. He'll be back.' She hung up. But, she'd already given hers."

Vikki's heart pounded faster. "What is it?"

CHAPTER SEVEN

"What's the person's name?" Angie asked.

Vikki was in the car driving with Gomez riding shotgun. Once Jody identified the caller, she searched the DMV database. Then called her friend, Angie Baxter, a journalist with the *St. Ives Examiner*, to pick her brain. Angie had perfected the art of poking her nose into other people's business without being intrusive.

"Her name is Susan Beverly. I have you on speaker."

"The over-the-hill actress?" asked Angie.

Vikki frowned. *"Over the Hill? Over the Hill.* I...I haven't seen that. Who else was in it?"

Gomez roared with laughter, clapping.

Angie let out an exasperated sigh. "Vikki, she's an actress, a bit older. She was in a few sitcoms in the late nineties. I hear she's trying to claw her way back in. It's rumored she's being considered for a major role as the matriarch in a family-friendly show on Netflix or Hulu."

Heat rushed to Vikki's cheeks. She hated being called out.

"Wait!" Angie said, drawing the word out. "The body found on the lake is linked to her?"

Vikki turned to Gomez. "You see, I told you. She knows everything that's happening in St. Ives."

"What did you say?" Angie asked.

"I was talking to Gomez, sorry—"

"Hello, Mike," Angie said. "Now, close your ears."

Gomez chuckled and wiped tears from his eyes. "I'll try."

Vikki continued. "Ms. Beverly called to report her partner missing on Friday evening."

"Missing?" Angie said. "He can't be missing. She's a puma or cougar. Let's see. Probably a cougar. Maybe *he* got tired and stepped out with someone closer to his age."

"I hope you don't mind—what's the difference?" Gomez asked.

Angie sighed. "These women seek out men at least ten years younger than them. Pumas are usually under forty, while cougars are women in their forties, fifties, and beyond."

"Ah, that clarifies things for me," Gomez said.

Vikki kept her eyes straight on the road, hands firmly on the wheel. "We don't even know it's the same guy. Maybe she's dating someone else. This is all speculation. Since she didn't call back, maybe he returned."

"Most people rarely call back," Gomez said in a low voice.

"Vikki—I have to go," Angie said. "Please keep me in the loop. I have to get back to a story I'm working on, but I'm yet to write on the swimming dead. Wow, Swimming Dead. That's an eye-catching headline. I'll call back to see if you have anything new."

Angie hung up.

A few minutes later, Vikki pulled up to the single-story building that housed Beverly Travel Agency. It reminded her of her dentist's clinic, an old house restored and retrofitted.

A huge glass window with a poster of a family running on an exotic beach was at the center of the glass. Vikki killed the engine in front of the office. She Googled who Susan Beverly was involved with. It returned Till Bruno. There was a picture further down. "Could that be our victim?"

Gomez squinted at her screen. "It's possible. I'll say ninety-seven percent." He turned and looked at the building. "This is a classic case of a career change. When one door closes, another one opens. I never knew the actress owned this place." He stepped out, bringing with him a folder with the sketch.

Vikki led the way into the office. The door opened into a compact office with three computer terminals. The walls were painted in different shades of blue. Posters of tourist locations—The Eiffel Tower, Big Ben, Niagara Falls, Egyptian pyramids—and places Vikki didn't know hung on the walls.

Only one of the three tables with a computer screen and chairs was occupied. The lady on it stood and approached them.

"Hi, I'm Maggie. How can I help you?" She was a tall black woman, neatly dressed in an electric-blue blouse tucked into a below-the-knee black skirt. Her large-rimmed glasses and braids tied in a bun gave her the appearance of a librarian. She smiled, revealing even white teeth.

Maggie's eyes darted back and forth between Vikki and Gomez, her gaze shifting rapidly between the two. "Let me guess. You're interested in an exotic romantic getaway?"

CHAPTER EIGHT

Vikki turned to the poster of the pyramids and pointed. "Maybe in the afterlife. After his wife sends us both there."

Gomez laughed. "I can't wait to share this with Selena. Maybe she'll ask me to quit today instead of in twelve months."

Vikki showed her badge. "I'm Detective Mattsen—my partner, Detective Gomez. We're here to see Susan Beverly."

Maggie stared at her shield, and her smile widened. "My bad." She pointed them to a waiting area with two chairs and some magazines. "Why don't you take a seat? I'll let her know you're here."

"Thanks," Vikki said and sat.

"And look around. Everyone needs an exotic vacation now and then." Maggie disappeared down a corridor, her feet silent on the carpeted floor.

Gomez picked up a magazine. "Nice gig. I wonder if she's *really* making money?"

"Why shouldn't she?"

"With all the online travel discount websites, with amazing deals, I wonder who goes to a place like this."

Vikki thought about it. "I guess you're right. Like book-stores, everyone has one destination in mind now."

Moments later, Maggi returned. "Ms. Beverly will see you."

She led them to a door, knocked once, and opened it. They stepped in.

Susan Beverly stood and walked to them. "Hello, Detectives." Her voice was deep, hoarse, like Bonnie Tyler's. There was a youthful bounce to her steps. She was trim and dressed smartly in a navy-blue skirt suit.

Her almost makeup-free face, Vikki knew, was once considered very beautiful. Her brown hair grazed her shoulders.

All that went through Vikki's head was: cougar. Vikki pegged her in her early fifties.

"That will be all for now, Maggie," Susan said. "Please." She pointed at the two chairs on the other side of the table. "How can I help you?"

Vikki brought out a small notepad from her pants pocket. She leaned forward. "Ms. Beverly, we—"

"Please, call me Susan."

"Susan." Vikki smiled and made a show of consulting her notes. "We received your call on Saturday evening and are following up. We presume Mr. Till Bruno made it back safely."

"Well, no," Susan said. She sighed, pursed her lips, and made a face like a parent being told their child had misbehaved in school. "Not yet."

"Not yet?" Vikki asked, fighting hard to control her facial expressions. A man who could very much be Till Bruno lay dead in the morgue. "Are you in touch with him?"

Ms. Beverly exhaled. "It's a long story. I'll explain. I was going to Times Square on Friday night for an event, and he didn't want to come. We had a spat, and I left without him.

When I came back, he wasn't home. And his phone has been switched off since then. I think he's cooling off somewhere."

"Cooling off? Why do you think that?" Gomez asked.

Vikki contained a smile, the irony not lost on her.

"Well, we've argued in the past, and he'd take off." A flush crossed Susan's cheeks. She appeared embarrassed. "See, Till is a lot younger than me. I think sometimes he'd rather not be seen with me in public." She shrugged. "My opinion—he disagrees. But I'm okay with that. He'll take off and come back when he feels better."

Vikki nodded. "Is he normally gone for this long?"

"No."

"But you waited until Saturday to report him missing."

"I heard the police only considered people missing only after it's twenty-four hours since you last saw them."

Vikki let out an exasperated groan. "That's another thing Hollywood gets wrong. The sooner the police are contacted, the better for a positive outcome." She glanced at Gomez. "Someone has to talk to those screenwriters."

Gomez opened a folder. "This morning, we pulled out the body of a young man in his mid-to-late twenties from the bottom of St. Ives Lake."

"He drowned?" Susan asked, her voice barely audible.

Gomez raised the sketch. "Yes. There was no ID on the individual, so we had an artist make a drawing. Do you by any chance know this person?"

Vikki's eyes were on Susan, watching out for false mannerisms. In instances like this, she tried to give everyone the benefit of the doubt, but her suspicions outweighed her compassion.

Susan looked. Her face turned the color of the inside of a cracked-open coconut.

Her knuckle flew to her mouth. She collapsed into her chair.

CHAPTER NINE

"Deep breaths, deep breaths," Gomez said as he fanned Susan with a folder.

Vikki was on her feet. "Are you okay?' She felt foolish as soon as the words left her mouth. You don't faint when you are okay. "I'll get you some water!"

"That's my Till...my Till. He's dead?"

Vikki pulled open the door and jerked back. Maggie stood there wide-eyed. Was she eavesdropping? Vikki recovered first. "Where can I get a glass of water for Ms. Beverly?"

Maggie stared, not responding.

Vikki placed her hands on her shoulders. "Water, for Ms. Beverly."

"At...at the...the break room. Follow me. What happened?"

"She'd identified Till Bruno as the drowning victim we found at the lake."

Maggie slowed. Her legs seemed to falter. She stopped and turned to Vikki. "What? Till dead?"

Vikki nodded. The break room was in sight. "I'm so sorry —you knew him?"

"Yes," Maggie said. Her voice filled with emotion. I-I'll get the water." She entered the break room, filled a plastic cup from the dispenser, and gave it to Vikki.

They both rushed back to the office.

Susan appeared more composed, with streaks of tears on her cheeks. She held the sketch.

Vikki passed her the water. "Here."

Susan reached for the cup, her hand shaking. She took a sip and put the glass down. "I think I'm okay. God, I need a cigarette. I'm trying to quit, you know." Her quivering lips attempted a smile. She pulled open a drawer and brought out a pack of Virginia slims and Nicorette gum.

Vikki felt sorry for her. Bad news threatened to reverse all progress she'd made in trying to quit.

Susan tried to open the pack of gum. "Are...are you guys sure it's him? He's an excellent swimmer. Was? Oh my God." She cried again. "I can't talk about him in the past tense." She squeezed the pack of gum tight, not opening it.

"The ME will still need to make an official identification," Vikki said. "Do you think you can come to the ME's office?"

Susan looked up sharply like she wasn't ready to see him yet.

Vikki noticed. "I don't mean to make this harder...there are other ways we can confirm his ID. Do you know which dentist he uses?"

"Dr. Masha. We use the same dentist. I'll give you his number." Susan picked up her phone. Her hands shook violently. She tried to scroll. Her fingers were not cooperating. "Where is it?" She let out a heavy sigh.

"We can get it later," Vikki said. She didn't want to make a bad situation worse. "Is there anyone we can call for you? Family or a close friend?"

Susan raised the cup to her lips, spilling some. "I think

I'm all right now...I was in shock." She glanced at a small table, balled her fist, and bit her knuckles.

Vikki followed her gaze. Framed pictures. She knew *exactly* how Susan felt. She'd been there. At the end of the day, all you had were memories. The photos were priceless. Time eased the hurt and pain but stole memories. Pictures kept those fading moments fresh.

At least Susan had pictures. Vikki hadn't bothered much with pictures growing up and had little of herself and Alexis. She looked at the framed photos of the happy couple. One at the Eiffel Tower, Paris. Another with Dubai's famous *Burj Al Arab* hotel as a backdrop. The last one was a picture of the happy couple, smiling on a beach and sipping wine. In the background was a long white building. At least they'd made good memories.

"Detective Mattsen?" Gomez said.

Vikki turned. "Yes?"

Gomez raised an eyebrow.

"Sorry," Vikki said. "Those pictures brought back memories." She fished in her pocket. "Susan, this is my card. You can call me when you are ready to visit the ME so we can plan. Again, I'm sorry for your loss."

Vikki and Gomez left her office for the reception area.

"They must have been close," Gomez said.

Vikki nodded. "It's a shame. Until the ME confirms a cause of death, what we have is possible accidental drowning. I wonder who will replace Patel?"

Gomez shrugged. "Who knows?"

Maggie was not in the reception area.

"I was hoping Maggie was here," Vikki said, tilting her head. She paused when she heard a sob and turned to Gomez. "Did you hear that?" she asked.

Gomez pointed. "Over there."

Maggie was sitting, doubled over, crying.

CHAPTER TEN

Vikki plucked some tissue from the box on the table and went to Maggie. "Here."

Maggie raised her head, showing bloodshot eyes.

"I'm so sorry for your loss. Maggie. We need your help. Anything you can tell us will be appreciated. We need to determine how he ended up in the lake. Can I ask you a few questions? "When was the last time you saw Till Bruno?"

Maggie hesitated. Her glance shifted from Vikki to Gomez and back to Vikki.

"Thursday afternoon, he was right here talking to Bruce."

Vikki's heart thudded. Her sweetheart had been Bruce, too. "Who's Bruce?"

Maggie's head was down. "My boyfriend."

"What happened next?" Gomez asked, taking a step closer.

"Bruce left. A few minutes later, Till and Ms. Beverly left, too."

Vikki pushed her hair behind her ear. "What did Bruce and Till talk about?"

Maggie thought for a moment and, shaking her head, said,

"Small talk. I wasn't paying attention. Till and Bruce hang out sometimes. I think they were going to meet up later and play pool."

"Did you know that for a fact? Did they?" Vikki asked.

Maggie raised an eyebrow. "Did they what?"

"Play pool?"

Maggie hesitated. "I know they met, but Bruce came home early. If I knew I wasn't going to see Till again, I'd have hung on to his every word." Her voice broke.

Vikki gave her a moment to regain her composure. She didn't want to go hard on her yet. She felt there was more to this than Maggie was letting on. "Where can we find Bruce?"

Maggie glanced at a wall clock with plane wings as hands. "Probably at the gym working out."

Vikki woke her iPhone with a tap on the screen, then put in the password. "What's the full name and address of the gym?"

Maggie's eyebrows narrowed. "Do you think Bruce has something to do with Till's drowning?"

"We don't know anything," Vikki said. "We're trying to piece together Mr. Bruno's whereabouts on that day, speak to the last person or persons that saw him alive, and build a timeline on what happened."

Maggie nodded. "It's Gym Bruce, twenty-seven Fulton Street."

Vikki typed the address into her phone's map app.

"Maggie, I'm going to ask you a few more questions," Gomez said. "Just routine. Where were you on Friday night between nine p.m. and twelve midnight?"

Maggie wiped her tears with the back of her hand. "I was home. I closed the office by five p.m. I stopped at the liquor store two doors away from here, bought two bottles of wine, then went home. I didn't leave the house until Saturday morning."

"Were you alone?" Gomez asked.

"Bruce came back—we live together, maybe around seven p.m. We ate, drank some wine, then slept. It was only Bruce and me."

"Okay, thank you very much," Vikki said, putting away her phone. She handed her a business card. "Please call me if there's anything you remember or you just want to talk."

Back in the car, Gomez said, "How convenient. The two people who saw Till last are each other's alibis."

"Let's pay Bruce a visit and hear his side of the story."

CHAPTER ELEVEN

Vikki would never have guessed a gym was under the hotel's parking lot. If she ever trained at this gym, she'd be constantly alert. What if the parking lot crashed and drowned them in concrete and asphalt?

A whiff of stale sweat, body odor, and urine welcomed them as they stepped in. Deep grunts, shouts of encouragement, and the metallic sound of clicking metal gave Vikki the impression that the gym was a guy's affair.

Who went to the gym by noon anyway? To her, exercise was something you did in the early morning or the evening.

A door to their right opened. The *boom-boom-boom* of loud music spilled out, plus women in sweat-soaked tank tops and cycling shorts, chatting amongst themselves. A sign above the door said Spinning Room.

"That was a good way to spend a lunch break," said one of the women.

Vikki saw sense in that. Not everyone had mornings or evenings free to work out. She agreed that riding a stationary bike was a practical way to meet your exercise quota. Yesterday and early this morning, she'd burned quite some calories with Ted. She pushed the thought away. He must have left town by now. Maybe she should take up spinning.

The gym rumbled. A heavy car with a big engine was overhead. She hoped this wasn't the day a car decided to dive through the roof.

A blonde in a black spandex top and bottom, probably in her early twenties, walked toward them from the reception counter, smiling.

"Hi, is this your first time?" Her eyes went from Vikki to Gomez.

Vikki smiled back. "Yes, it is." She followed up before the next apparent questions were asked. "I'm Detective Mattsen, my partner, Detective Gomez—we were told we would find Bruce here."

"He's here," said Ms. Spandex. "I'll take you to him. Come."

She led them past a bar. Men and women stood, waiting for their turn to order or pick up their drinks. The sound of a blender, music, and a TV gave it the feel of being in an indoor sporting event.

Ms. Spandex stopped and watched a man in a sleeveless tee shirt with bulging biceps. She nodded in his direction and whispered in Vikki's ear, "Bruce."

Bruce leaned over another man doing bench presses with weights that looked like Mini Coopers on each side. The man's face was so contorted that it seemed like he needed fiber in his diet.

"Almost there, push!" Bruce said. He put a finger under the bar and helped the man stretch his hand. He then guided him to place the bar safely on the support beams.

All the while, Vikki was saying to herself: *This guy can subdue a buffalo. Add motive, and we'll have a suspect.*

"Bruce, the police are here to see you," said Ms. Spandex as if it were a regular occurrence.

"Hi, guys!" Bruce said, turning around. He didn't miss a beat. "How can I help you?"

Gomez extended his hand and introduced them.

Bruce shook his hand, then Vikki's. "It's a pleasure to meet you, too," he said.

Vikki felt his every callous. She was glad he didn't squeeze as some knuckleheads did.

"Do you have a quiet place where we can talk?" Gomez asked.

Bruce paused for a second. "Sure—my office."

Bruce's office was a glorified storage room with three chairs, two treadmills, an elliptical, and some archaic bikes.

"So, how can I help you, Detectives?" Bruce asked.

He sat on a chair, arms resting on his thighs, biceps bulging. He reminded Vikki of the old cartoon *Popeye the Sailor Man*, the spinach eater.

"We were at Beverly Travel Agency," Gomez said. "We were told you'd be here. We have a few questions about Friday night."

"What about Friday?"

Vikki raised an eyebrow. "Did you see Till Bruno on Friday?"

Bruce was perplexed. "Yes, of course, at the agency."

"What did you guys talk about?" Gomez asked.

Bruce pursed his lips and shrugged. "I don't know. It's not like we were having a board meeting. It was more like running into each other."

"Do you run into each other that often?" Gomez continued.

Bruce pumped his hand in the air, palms out. "Hold on, hold on. I've seen enough *Law and Order* reruns to know you're not interested in my social life. Why don't you come clean and ask me what you want to know?"

"Okay," Vikki said with a cock of her head. "Where were you between nine p.m. and midnight on Friday?"

"That's easy. I was home in bed with my girlfriend. We ate, indulged in some wine, and retired. Why?"

"It's about Till Bruno," said Vikki. "He's—"

"His old lady's looking for him?" Bruce said, cutting her off.

A tinge of excitement ran down Vikki's spine. "What do you know about that?"

CHAPTER TWELVE

Bruce exhaled and said, "Sometimes he'd rather not be seen with her in public—and they have these arguments." He smiled.

Vikki opened her palm. "Do you want to share what's funny?"

Bruce chuckled. "His job is to be Mr. Susan Beverly. Who cares if she'd pass for his mother? They're in a mutually beneficial relationship. She gets the stud. He gets the famous actress—plus financial stability. That's a cushy job. How hard could it be?"

"Who knows," Gomez said. "Maybe he doesn't see it that way."

"I don't understand why he'd rather not be seen with her in public," Bruce said, shaking his head. "One of these days, I'm going to break his neck and toss him in the lake. I don't know why Susan called you guys. Till will be back." "Till—Will. Get it?"

"No, he won't," Gomez said. "He was fished out of Lake St. Ives this morning."

The smile on Bruce's face faded. "What? Till is dead?"

Vikki nodded. "And your story doesn't add up to what we heard. You conveniently omitted the fact that you guys played pool that night. You were the last person seen with him alive."

Bruce raised both hands. "Hold...hold on. I did not kill anybody." Beads of sweat dotted his forehead. He spoke fast. "We hung out at The Shack. Played pool over a few drinks to get in the mood, then his phone rang."

Vikki wanted to ask what getting in the mood meant, but she saved it. It was never a good idea to interrupt a suspect providing information.

"And?" Gomez asked.

"He stepped away from me and answered. When he hung up, he said he had to go."

Vikki gestured with her hands. "Did he say who called?"

Bruce shook his head slowly. "Nope. A similar thing happened on Thursday, too. About the same time."

Vikki raised her eyebrows. "Thursday, too?"

"Yes, he left in the middle of the pool game. So, I finished the game, paid my bill, and left. In the parking lot, I saw him talking to a man."

"Can you give us a description?"

Bruce threw out his hands. "White, average height, and he had a baseball hat on. He and Till were arguing—I didn't join them. Sometimes it's better to keep your nose where it belongs."

Gomez took out a small notebook from his pocket. "What time was this?"

Bruce shrugged. "Seven or seven-thirty. The time should be on my tab."

"So that was Thursday," Vikki said. "What about Friday?"

"I saw Till last at the travel agency on Friday. He didn't show up. His phone was switched off, so I went home to Maggie."

"You said you were drinking to get in the mood," Gomez said. "Mood for what?"

Bruce took a deep breath. He lowered his head and expelled it slowly from his mouth. "There's no way to sugar-coat this. Erm...Till was supposed to come home with me. He...he and Maggie would have something going...while... while I watched."

It was like he'd dropped a bomb. Everything went still.

Gomez recovered first. "And you were okay with that?"

Bruce said nothing.

Gomez shrugged. "Okay, I get it. Some people smoke pot to get high. Some others get there from being around them. Firsthand or secondhand smoke—same destination."

Vikki cleared her throat. "Back to the parking lot. Can you think of anything else to help identify this man?"

Bruce jutted out his lower lip. He thought for a moment, then snapped his fingers. "Hell, I can show you."

CHAPTER THIRTEEN

"It must have recorded them," Bruce said.

Vikki was glad they didn't need to drive. His idea was the CCTV cameras facing The Shack's parking lot located nearby. It was the bar at the hotel Bruce had his gym. They'd flashed their badges, and the manager, a twenty-something-year-old man with a ponytail, was very cooperative. He recognized Gomez from seeing him around St. Ives since he was a kid.

"Good thing this wasn't ten years ago," said the manager.

Still smiling from being recognized, Gomez said, "Why's that?"

"Thank God for cloud computing. Then, we still had VCRs and probably recorded over the footage."

Back in the detective squad room twenty minutes later, Vikki sat behind her computer and focused on the footage from The shack.

The camera was focused on the entrance and got little of the parking lot. Vikki watched at regular speed and fast-forwarded once she recognized Bruce and Till walking into The Shack.

It wasn't lost on Vikki that the man on the screen was already dead.

Did he have premonitions about his death? It was an inevitable end for everyone. To her, it was better not to know than to know.

Her mind drifted to twelve years ago, and she had to reel it back. Right on time, too, or she might have missed Till when he came out of the bar. The date and time on the recording were in white text at the bottom of the screen.

Till glanced around, then turned to his right as if someone had called him. The video was grainy, even with today's technology.

Gomez had explained that most videos recorded boring noncriminal activity, so blurry and monochromatic was the cheapest way to record and store them.

"The higher the video quality, the more expensive the camera and the more storage space you need."

A figure in the shadows between parked cars waved Till over.

"Please show your face," Vikki murmured.

Till came closer and closer. Vikki licked her lips in anticipation.

As Till got closer, the man emerged from the shadows. He pointed to his left, and they both took off in that direction. Vikki groaned.

Gomez returned and flopped into his seat. "Any luck?"

Vikki clicked on the back button. "The man Till met appeared at six-ten p.m. I don't know if this view is good enough." She paused it. "Here."

Gomez squinted. "I think it will do. People have been identified with worse. Maybe James at IT forensics can put their facial recognition AI on it and come up with a match."

Vikki took in a cleansing breath and let it out slowly. Her

mode improved. "You should be nicer and stop harassing them."

"It's horsing around," Gomez said.

Vikki held the thumb drive like a priest about to deliver communion and went over to James Madden's desk, one of SIPD's resident geeks. Gomez followed.

James smiled. "Detective Mattsen, what do you have for me?"

"Facial recognition expertise," Gomez said. "Where's the other apostle?"

James' smile vanished. "This time, we'll call security on you. Someone is where they shouldn't be."

Vikki pushed the thumb drive to James. "He's trying to be funny. Don't pay attention to him. We need your help. We have a person of interest we'd like to identify. He appears on Thursday, six-ten p.m."

James took the drive from Vikki, then glared at Gomez. He inserted it into his computer and typed out some commands. The video came on, and he paused it at the designated time. "Now, I'll set the software on your image."

Vikki watched with fascination as faces flashed and disappeared on James' computer screen.

Five minutes later, he said, "Mark Darnel."

··

CHAPTER FOURTEEN

··

Vikki felt like a weight had been removed from her shoulders. Finally, they were getting somewhere. "Any information about this Mark Darnel?"

James let out a breath and nodded. "He's spending time as a guest of Florida State at one of its free accommodation facilities."

Vikki stood beside James Madden's chair, looking at his screen. "Is that for real? That was fast."

James chuckled and shut off the video. "Florida has one of the country's most advanced facial recognition databases. It made sense to start there, and we got lucky." He handed the drive back to Vikki.

Gomez took a sticky note and pen from Madden's desk and wrote the name. "I'll run his financials and see what we can find."

"Thanks so much," Vikki said. She left the office and went to the break room. She got a bottle of iced lemon tea from the vending machine. Vikki drank half the bottle on her way back to her desk. It was refreshing.

At her desk, she printed out Mark Darnel's mugshot. He

looked older than Till. How had they met? What was the connection?

Vikki checked Till Bruno against the law enforcement database to see if he had any criminal records. The system spat out results. "What do we have here?" she said in a low voice, piecing the information together in her head to make sense as she read.

Till Bruno had had a troubled youth. A graduate of the foster home system. Bounced from one family to another, he was never loved. Someone had written in a scanned document.

He excelled in math and coding as a kid. Along the way, he'd picked up other skills like lying, burglary, and computer hacking and spent a year in a Florida jail for cyberbullying. *Cyberbullying?*

Till had a knack for computers, but he'd used his skills to commit crimes. He'd been caught breaking the law, charged, and jailed.

Vikki dug deeper. She found out the name of the detective in charge of the case and called him in Tampa—Detective Cole.

"Cole speaking, who's this?"

Vikki explained who she was and why she was calling.

"What's your name again?"

Vikki told him.

"Bye." He hung up.

"Hello." Vikki stared at her phone. "What the...?" A few seconds later, the phone on Vikki's table rang. She snatched it. "Detective Mattsen."

"This is Cole. Sorry, I had to confirm your bona fide. You said Till Bruno drowned? Accidental drowning?"

"Drowned, yes, but we're still investigating."

"What a waste. He could have become another Zuckerberg, Jobs, or Gates if he'd applied his skills to noncriminal endeavors. Sad to hear. How can I help you?"

"Yes. I came across the cyberbullying conviction, and I thought perhaps you can provide more insight on what happened."

"Sure," said Cole. "He and another man, his name escapes me right now, fleeced retirees off their life savings. Till used his skills to hack into their computers and steal information, then empty their accounts. If hacking didn't work, they used verbal threats. They were successful until we set up a sting operation and nabbed them."

"How old was Mr. Bruno then?"

"He'd turned twenty-one. He made a deal with the prosecutor and was charged with a cyberbullying misdemeanor instead of a felony. One year if convicted instead of five."

Vikki exhaled. "What was the deal?" She had a sinking feeling in the pit of her stomach. A sense their working diagnosis of accidental drowning was resting on rocky feet and might turn into a homicide.

"Give up his accomplices. It was a ring, but Till dealt with one guy...yes, Mark! Mark Darnel. We got them all." There was a pause. "I think Darnel got the least number of years—five. He should be out about now for good behavior. That is, assuming he behaved while in the can."

Another pause.

"Is he somehow connected to Till's drowning?"

Vikki exhaled. "The night before Mr. Bruno allegedly drowned, he was seen arguing with a man in the parking lot of a hotel who we identified as Mark Darnel."

"No shit. Anyway, I have to go. If you have any more questions, don't hesitate to call."

Vikki thanked him and hung up. Now they had to find Mark Darnel.

CHAPTER FIFTEEN

Vikki sat at her desk, oblivious to activities going on around her in the detective squad room. She stared at the monitor, not seeing it. Elbows resting on her desk, her hands clasped together, she tapped her lower lip. Till Bruno's early life wasn't that distant from hers. She'd lost her parents at a young age, a foster home, and lost people who'd cared for her.

A stapled document landed on her table. Vikki gasped and jerked back.

"Sorry, I didn't mean to startle you," Gomez said. "I picked this up from the printer. It seems like Mark Darnel got out early from a five-year jail term. And right away, he goes looking for his protégé."

Vikki snatched the document and flipped through it. "I spoke with Detective Cole in Tampa. He was in charge of the case Till was arrested and jailed for when he was twenty-one. He gave me a summary."

"It seems like they have unfinished business," Gomez said. "Maybe Till kept back some of the loot. Or Darnel came back to continue where they left off, and Till said no. He's getting his life together and has learned his lesson. Darnel won't take no for an answer. He's frustrated and, in a rage, murders Till."

Vikki threw open her hands. "How? There wasn't any evidence of foul play." She took a deep breath and exhaled in a rush. "Not having an ME is a handicap. At least we should have had some concrete answers by now on what caused his death. We must find Darnel. He's the key to what happened to Till."

Gomez pointed at the documents in Vikki's hands. "I pulled his financials too. He deposited twenty-five thousand dollars into his account last Tuesday. Here in St. Ives. Prior to that, he had only a few hundred dollars in it."

"That's a great leap. We can trace where it came from."

"He's smarter than we think. He walked into the bank and deposited it in cash," Gomez said.

"Maybe he got it from Till."

Gomez shook his head. "I ran his financials, too. No withdrawals to that amount. He has about ten grand."

"Or, someone who owed him money paid up."

Gomez shrugged. "Who knows? At least he's leaving breadcrumbs we can follow. According to his credit card statement, he rented a car from Newark Airport on Sunday. He probably flew in. I'll call Avis to find out the make and model of his vehicle and put out a BOLO."

"Any hits on accommodation?"

"He must have paid cash somewhere. Many prefer cash."

Vikki's cell phone rang. It was Angie. "I'll take this."

"Go ahead. I have a few calls to make."

"What happened, Vikki?" Angie asked. "You didn't call me back. So, what did you find out?"

"I'm at my desk right now." Vikki hoped Angie picked up the cue.

"Okay, answer yes or no. Was it Susan Beverly's husband?"

Vikki answered in the affirmative.

"Oh, that is so sad. I was researching her, and things had begun to turn around for her. She grew up poor—paid her way through acting school. She was a waitress for a long time. Then came the role that put her in the limelight. After that flash-in-the-pan success, things dried up."

"Isn't that how it happens for most actors trying to break in?"

"Yes, but she just got this new role," Angie said. "The light at the end of the tunnel and the biggest for her career. Found the man of her dreams, and he drowns. So sad. Is there anything you can add to that?"

Vikki was supposed to say no. Instead, she said, "Not yet. We're still looking into her husband's past. Things might not be as straightforward as we think."

"Scandalous. Can I print that?"

"Hold your horses. I'll let you know when and what, okay?" Vikki's landline rang. "I have to go." She hung up and picked up the phone.

"Mattsen."

"Detective Mattsen?" said a voice that sounded like something computer generated.

"Yes."

"I'm Dr. Stuart. I'm here temporarily at the ME's office. Could you drop by when you have a second? It's about your drowning case."

"Sure. I'll be right there."

Vikki glanced at Gomez. He was still on the phone. She mouthed, "ME."

His eyes widened. He moved the mouthpiece of his phone. "They found a new one already. Who?"

Vikki gathered the documents on her table. "Your guess is as good as mine. Let's go find out."

"You go ahead. I'm not ready yet to see another person in Amitab's position."

Vikki shook her head and left.

CHAPTER SIXTEEN

Vikki entered the morgue. The smell of embalming fluid was stronger than usual. She stopped at the changing area. The morgue was as cold as the frozen food section at the grocery store on a summer day. She shivered, goosebumps appearing all over her skin.

She grabbed the protective coverall from the shelf, stepped into it, and pulled it over her pantsuit. She then donned shoe covers, a mask, and gloves and secured her hair. Hoping the gear would protect her from the cold, she entered the morgue.

A man in protective autopsy regalia stood over a body on the autopsy table. Maybe he hadn't heard her come in with the constant humming of the refrigerators.

He studied the body. Its torso was exposed, showing a Y-shaped incision. The patient's arms were at odd angles, with broken bones protruding through the skin. The lower part of the patient was modestly covered with a white sheet, with bulges suggesting broken bones, too. Vikki swallowed. She'd never get used to this.

"Dr. Stuart?"

The man's head shot up.

"Detective Mattsen? Sorry, I didn't hear you come in." He smiled and raised gloved hands. "There won't be any hand-shaking."

Vikki smiled. "Fine with me."

Dr. Stuart exhaled. "Sorry for interrupting your day. I thought I should explain to you in person the situation I'm facing here. I won't be spending much time here. I got pulled in from the county hospital to help out. I understand you're waiting on a patient."

Vikki nodded.

"I have good news, though. They found a pathologist who should be coming in soon to take over on a more permanent basis."

"Great... How soon?"

His shoulders sagged. "They didn't tell me that. But I presume in a few hours."

"Nice," said Vikki, but she needed answers, like yesterday.

"I did the autopsies on a first come, first served basis. The new guy will do the next patient when he comes in. I didn't want to start what I won't finish."

Vikki hid her disappointment. "I was hoping to get a preliminary time of death for the drowned victim to help with the investigation."

Dr. Stuart sighed. "Having an accurate time of death for drowned victims is tricky because they've been in water for some time. I know the technician made a rough assessment of forty-eight hours from when he saw him this morning. I'll echo that."

Vikki was not a fan of gawking at dead bodies, but there was something familiar about the man lying on the table.

Dr. Stuart cocked his head. Looked at her, then at the patient. "He was in a car that was hit by a train."

Vikki had heard about the train accident in passing. Then, they were still wrapped up in who knew what.

It was one of those freight trains that traveled mostly at night. There was no explosion or other cars involved. But, Jesus, being hit by a train. She made a face—no wonder the arms and legs went in every direction.

Dr. Stuart chuckled. "The morgue is not for the faint of heart." He clasped his hands together. "Anyway, that's it."

Vikki wasn't happy he'd asked her to come down to tell her he wouldn't be working on her case. She was still polite. "I'll come back later and see the new pathologist. Thanks for the heads-up."

"It was a pleasure meeting you," Dr. Stuart said. "I thought I should tell you how things stand and apologize in person."

"That was nice of you. I appreciate it." Vikki left but still had a nagging feeling about the body on the table.

Vikki returned to the office. Gomez was gone. She didn't blame him... Considering that he'd woken up early to take Dr. Patel to the airport.

There were no leads to chase down. Tired, she packed her things and left.

At her place, she soaked in her bathtub and relaxed her body and mind. She had dinner, leftover chicken and rice, then went to bed.

Vikki bolted up soon after she'd shut her eyes. She'd remembered where she'd seen the face on the autopsy table previously. She couldn't wait for the day to break.

CHAPTER SEVENTEEN

Vikki rushed into the office the next morning. She dropped her handbag at her desk and headed for the ME's office. She had to confirm what she thought she'd seen. She'd sent a text to Gomez to meet her at the morgue.

Vikki put protective clothing over her pantsuit and went in. A quick look around told her Gomez wasn't there yet.

Like yesterday, another doctor in scrubs and protective clothing worked on a body on the table with his back to her. Not Dr. Stuart. This doctor was taller, broad-shouldered, and bigger.

A chill ran down Vikki's spine. He was working on Till Bruno. He slowly cut in a line from behind one ear to the other, passing over the forehead. Then, he separated the cut into two halves and peeled them back from the skull like flaps of skin. The front flap he draped over the corpse's face, and the rear flap was pulled over its neck.

Vikki wished she'd come at another time. For her, it was better to visit the morgue when the autopsy was done. The doctor picked up an electric saw and turned it on. The sound changed from a whine to a grating sound when he cut into the patient's skull.

The examiner turned the saw off and looked over his shoulder. He did a double take, then placed the saw down.

"Vikki!"

Vikki leaned forward. His protective goggles and face mask made it tough to figure out who he was.

"Ted?" Her head shot back, eyes wide. "Ted, you're still here? What...what are you doing here?"

Ted laughed. "Autopsy."

Vikki shook her head. "I-I mean. You know what I mean. I thought you'd be long gone to—to wherever."

"Well, I was still in the area when I got an alert about a forensic pathologist job opening. I like St. Ives. I have a special friend here." Ted raised a shoulder. "And I said, why not?"

Vikki stared, her heart beating like she was on a roller coaster right at the first drop. "You are the last person I expected to see." She inhaled and exhaled. "So it was you Dr. Stuart was talking about yesterday."

Ted laughed. "As I said, I saw the opportunity online. St. Ives is growing on me, and I'll be closer to you."

This was not what Vikki wanted to hear. "We should have at least discussed it." He was supposed to have moved on. Too much of a good thing was always bad. Moreover, she didn't get her cheese from the same place she got her milk.

Vikki exhaled. She'd have to deal with this later. She had a job to do.

Ted cocked his head and removed the safety goggles and facemask. The corners of his eyes crinkled when he smiled. "You don't seem happy to see me?"

"Yes. No...no, not that. More surprised. I didn't think in my wildest dreams you'd still be around."

Ted stared at her, his smile fading. He broke eye contact

and spread out his hands. "Okay, Detective Mattsen, Dr. Edward Brandon at your service. How can I help you?"

"I was waiting for you to ask."

Ted chuckled, shaking his head.

Vikki pointed at Till Bruno's fingers. "What do you think happened to his fingerprints? You think fish did that?"

"Maybe, but—" Ted picked up the patient's hand and isolated a finger. "It' seems like it was burned with a hot object like an electric iron. Then fish or whatever made it worse."

"Maybe somebody was trying to prevent him from getting fingerprinted and identified."

"Possible," Ted said. "What else can I help you with?"

Vikki looked down at her hands and rifled through the documents from yesterday. She picked out one and raised it for Ted to see. "Mark Darnel—do you recognize him?"

Ted leaned forward, removed his gloves and took the paper. "A mug shot." He pursed his lips. "Yes. I think I put him away in the freezer."

CHAPTER EIGHTEEN

Vikki managed to control herself from doing a victory lap. So she was right.

"According to Stuart, he had no ID." Ted glanced at the freezer that contained the bodies. "His car was hit by a train. Stuart hadn't gotten to him yet, so that's my next one. Is he one of your cases?"

Vikki exhaled. "He's a person of interest in figuring out what happened to Till, the drowned victim."

"Him?" Ted pointed at the body on the table and shook his head. "It can't be possible."

"Why not?"

"Darnel was brought in on Thursday from the train wreck, already dead. Till went missing on Friday."

The door to the examining room burst open.

Gomez rushed in dressed in a black suit, white shirt, and blue striped tie. He stopped when he saw them. "Oops." He backtracked.

"Sometimes he forgets to put on protective clothing," Vikki said.

Ted smiled. "Aren't we all guilty? It's happened to me too."

Gomez came in half a minute later. His face brightened as he came closer. "Ted! My God. I thought you left town?"

"Ah, Dr. Brandon—taking over from Dr. Patel. I thought of you as more of a private investigator than an ME. You know, from the Appleton case. But this is good." He turned to Vikki, nodding. "Good, right? I got your text. What's going on?"

"Remember Mark Darnel?" Vikki said.

Gomez raised a shoulder. "Of course. Everybody is searching for him. The BOLO hasn't returned anything yet."

"Well, I found him." Vikki pointed at the body.

Gomes's eyebrows furrowed. "He's dead? How did that happen?"

Vikki told him about the accident.

Gomez took a deep breath and blew it out threw his mouth. "Jesus. now that our main suspect is dead, where do we go from here?" He shook his head.

Vikki nodded. "This is getting complicated. Darnel was deposited here from the train accident on Thursday. So he died on Thursday and Till on Friday. Well, Till was last seen alive on Friday. His body recovered on Monday."

"The question is, what happened?" Gomez said. "Darnel got in an accident, and Till accidentally drowned."

Vikki cocked her head. "How did the two of them manage to get themselves killed in accidents?"

Ted smiled and said, "I don't know the answer to that, but I'm waiting for the toxicology and lab reports from patient Till Bruno. I'll call you as soon as I have them. They might help."

Nobody spoke for a few seconds. Like a ghost had graced the occasion.

"Okay," Vikki said.

Ted snapped his fingers. "I nearly forgot." He walked over to a stainless-steel trolley with dissecting tools and picked up an evidence bag. "I found this clutched in the patient Darnel's, the train guy's, right hand." He handed the evidence bag to Vikki.

Vikki turned it around. Inside was a matchbox. She read out loud the text on it. "Leisure Tavern."

Gomez made a *gimme* sign. "I'll hand it over to CSU. They might still be able to get some prints from it."

"It might be his prints only," said Vikki. "After that, we'll drop by the Tavern and see if our victim was ever there."

CHAPTER NINETEEN

Vikki's mind was on autopilot as she drove toward Leisure Tavern. It was a location that had changed name and ownership over the years. She knew the general direction—go all the way down Main Street until it was Main Street no more.

Google had given her the street address. Vikki had a general idea about the building. She'd passed it a few times. But she called her journalist friend to get the behind-the-scenes story.

"The owner is ex-military. Don't ask, don't tell variety," said Angie. "You'll have to give me something. While I was waiting for you, someone else broke the story and the link to Susan Beverly. Can I mention this angle?"

Vikki wondered if she was already saying too much to her journalist friend. "Angie, we're on our way to the Tavern. We don't even know if there's any connection there. Hang on and trust me. I'll give you something interesting once we're done with the Tavern. Bye for now." Vikki hung up.

"Ms. Baxter is like a radio still working after the battery has been taken out," Gomez said. "Tough balancing act, but you're doing great."

Vikki ran through what they had in her mind. Yesterday, Till Bruno's body had been found in the lake. Questions had led to Bruce and then to Darnel. An ex-con who seemed to have unfinished business with the deceased. They started a search for him.

They found him all right.

On their way to Leisure Tavern, about twenty minutes from the PD., Gomez said, "This is uncanny. Finding our suspect dead right next to the victim. If only the dead could talk."

She'd heard Gomez, but her mind had drifted to Ted. Seeing him as the temporary ME had thrown her off. She didn't need that complication in her life.

Vikki's cell phone, suspended on the dash, rang. It was Captain Levin. She tapped the screen and put it on speaker. "Good morning, Captain."

"Mattsen. I thought I'd catch you in the office. You and Gomez are running late?"

"Morning, Captain," Gomez said.

"Gomez?"

"Yes, sir. We came in early to see the ME." Gomez checked the time on his watch. "We left the morgue about ten minutes ago. We're chasing down a lead."

"Good. That means you two have already met the new medical examiner. Bring me up to speed, Mattsen."

Vikki mentioned that the ME also thought the injury on the drowning victim's fingertips might have been malicious to delay or hide the victim's ID. She also talked about 'a person of interest' to the case they'd discovered in the morgue.

"Like, dead?" Captain Levin asked.

"Yes, sir," Gomez said.

"You already met the new examiner? A man of many skills. I like him. Down to earth, considering his accomplishments."

Vikki made a face. She'd deal with Ted later. Right now, she had two dead bodies to deal with.

"Try and get this wrapped up as soon as possible. The mayor is breathing down my neck. We need to get answers soon. I'll delay my press conference to later in the day. The narrative was more manageable when it appeared to be an unintentional drowning. No one to hold accountable. But now…"

"We'll get back to you as soon as we get something, sir," Vikki said.

The captain hung up without saying goodbye.

The further they drove out of town, the more the spaces between the houses got. Soon, they reached their destination. Vikki pulled into the empty parking lot.

Gomez glanced around the car park at the Tavern. "Where's everybody? It's always a full house whenever I drive past here."

Vikki parked next to a black Ford F-150 truck with Leisure Tavern in bold yellow text on the side. Excellent advertising. "It's only ten a.m. We'll be lucky if we find anybody here. It's more of a nocturnal venue."

Gomez got out of the car. "Let's hope the owner lives in the loft. It looks like one of those repurposed farmhouses." He walked to a side door and knocked. Then saw the bell. He pushed it, too.

By the third ring, footsteps approached the door from the inside.

CHAPTER TWENTY

The door opened. A bald man, probably in his thirties, peered through, tying the belt to his robe. He had a thick red beard—the type favored by the Taliban—but now the new fashion statement amongst young men. The faint smell of stale beer and cigarette smoke leached out of him.

Vikki flashed her badge and introduced themselves. "Peter Grant?"

The man shielded his eyes from the sun. "Jesus. I only went to bed a few hours ago." He had a gruff Brooklyn accent. "Yes, I'm Peter Grant, the owner. What's this all about?"

Vikki held her breath, glad it was only alcohol-infused dragon breath that came from him. "We're investigating a case, and we believe the persons of interest visited your facility. We have a few questions."

Peter Grant groaned. "Drunk driving? That's a long stretch. Most of my customers are locals, and I drop them off when they imbibe too much. Do you have a picture?"

Gomez handed him both pictures.

Vikki hoped he would invite them in. The ten a.m. sun was beginning to burn.

Peter Grant raised the photos one after the other. He shook his head. "I've never seen them."

"Do you remember everyone who comes to your bar?" Gomez asked.

"Yes. As I said, they're mostly locals. New faces stand out. What day was this?"

"Probably between Sunday and Thursday," Vikki said.

Peter Grant drew a sharp breath and dropped his head as he exhaled. "That explains it," he muttered. "I was out of town Sunday to Friday. I'll get my partner. He was here." He stepped back in and locked the door.

A few minutes passed.

Gomez turned to Vikki. "You think he's coming back?"

"Why not? Didn't you hear him?"

Five minutes later, Vikki reached for the bel and stopped. Someone was coming. The door opened, and a man, about five feet six inches in boxer shorts—no shirt—stepped out.

"Okay, fellas. Where are the pictures?" He had a singsong voice and waved his hands in the air with the passion of a symphony conductor.

Gomez's gaze flicked to Vikki and then back again. "And what's your name?" he said, clearing his throat.

Grant's partner locked eyes with Gomez for a few seconds. He licked a finger and pointed at him. "Anything you want it to be. Wow, you have nice thick eyebrows."

Gomez changed color. He'd pass for a beetroot with a blue striped tie wound around it.

Vikki intervened. "Have you come across any of them in the bar?"

"Hmm," said Grant's partner. "Monday night, this guy came in first and sat at the bar nursing a drink." He pointed at Mark Darnel. "Then this one joined." He pointed at Till Bruno.

"That's Till Bruno," said Gomez, regaining his demeanor.

"It was like a reunion. They were happy to see each other. I figured maybe one went away for a long time."

Adrenaline coursed through Vikki. "What happened next?"

"They had a few drinks, then left. Tuesday night, they came back. Till wasn't as happy as he was on the previous visit. They sat by the bar, talking."

"Did you get what they were talking about?" Vikki asked.

"Not really. Bits and pieces. Money and woman. At a point, an angry Till said he had no money. That's about it."

Vikki's phone rang. It was the ME. She raised the phone to answer, then groaned. It wasn't Dr. Patel anymore. Was that her new normal? "Detective Mattsen."

"Hello, this is Dr. Brandon. Concerning Mr. Darnel, the train accident victim, there are some new findings that I need to show you."

Vikki's heart raced. Perhaps this was the break they'd been waiting for. we'll be there in thirty minutes."

CHAPTER TWENTY-ONE

"Thank God for that phone call," Gomez said. "I needed to get out of there. That guy was breathing down my neck."

Vikki laughed. "He wasn't. I was there, too. He's a good-looking guy. You were scared he might convince you to play for the other team."

Vikki expected a comeback, but Gomez remained quiet. She stole a glance at Gomez. He was quiet. Maybe she'd hit a nerve. She changed the subject. "I wonder what Ted—Dr. Brandon—found out that he needs to show us."

"I wonder, too," Gomez said. "I was surprised to see him. It's a good thing, right?" A beat passed. "You don't seem excited."

It was Vikki's turn for silence. Gomez didn't push it.

They went straight to the morgue from the police station's car park. Vikki recognized Mark Darnel on the autopsy table. Dr. Brandon was all business.

"On visual examination, it was obvious there was some injury to the back of the head." He waved his gloved hand up and down the man's broken arms and legs. "He was already dead before all this."

Vikki nodded slowly. "The injuries didn't bleed."

"Exactly. When someone's alive, their heart pumps blood all over the body."

Vikki was aware but didn't interrupt him. She didn't want to appear dismissive.

"Any injury, especially of this magnitude, should bleed. But when I examined the patient—zilch."

"You think it was foul play?" Vikki asked.

Ted winked at Vikki. "That's the detective's job. Evidence shows he was already dead before impact with the train. Most of the bleeding was in his head. A blunt force trauma to the back of the head did him in."

Gomez frowned. "Maybe all the injuries happened when the train struck the car?"

"It's possible. The damage or injuries from an impact with a speeding train occurs in seconds, and all should bleed almost at the same time. But not in this case."

"Makes sense," Gomez said, nodding.

"The cause of death was from this." Dr. Brandon pointed to the head.

"What about the time of death?" Vikki asked.

"From Dr. Patel's notes, he placed his death between seven and ten p.m. Thursday when he saw him. Based on liver temperature and lividity. He even placed an asterisk on it—like something he wanted to revisit. The train driver said the impact was around nine p.m."

"Maybe Till murdered Darnel," Vikki said.

Gomez folded his hands over his chest. "Why? What's his motive?"

"Come on, pick one. They're many," Vikki said. "We discussed it when we thought Darnel murdered Till, now it's flipped. Maybe Darnel wanted to do a job with Till, and Till said no. Till's life is stable and good, and he has too much to lose. They argued. Things get out of hand. Till kills Darnel.

He placed his car on tracks to look like an accident. The next day, he was full of remorse and decided to commit suicide. He took something to incapacitate himself and went for a swim."

Ted cocked his head, glanced at Vikki, and nodded. "It's plausible. You're the detective. I've already ordered a toxicology report on Till Bruno, which should help your theory if it comes back with something. I'm curious, too. I'll call once I get the result."

Vikki and Gomez headed back to the police department.

CHAPTER TWENTY-TWO

Jody called out to Vikki and Gomez as they passed her. She was on the phone and covered the mouthpiece. "Hey, the captain wants to see you guys in his office, pronto!" She made a helpless gesture with her free hand. "The phones have been busy all morning."

Vikki gave her a sympathetic smile. She felt the same way. They needed more clues. "Did anyone examine Darnel's rental?"

Gomez shook his head.

"I think we should inspect Darnel's vehicle and visit the accident site," Vikki said as they waited for the elevator. "Maybe something was overlooked. Do you know who was first at the scene?"

Gomez pursed his lips. "I don't know which officers were first, but Mallory and his crew must have been there. He's good. I'm sure they did a thorough job."

Dennis Mallory headed the CSU of SIPD. A former homicide detective himself, he never left any stone unturned.

Vikki knocked once and opened the door to the captain's

office. He was on the phone but waved them in. He pointed to the chairs on the opposite side of his table.

Captain Levin concluded his call and turned to them. "That was the mayor. What do you have?"

Vikki summarized the findings to him. "We just came from talking to the owners of the bar where Till and Darnel had met. One of them overheard a situation that seemed like blackmail. This is what we've deduced so far. Mark Darlene is released from jail, and he visits his old pal. Their reunion goes well. He asks Till for a handout. We think Till gave him twenty-five thousand dollars."

"We pulled Darnel's statement, and the money was there," Gomez said. "We think he wanted more money, and Till must have said no. The bartender believes the relationship went downhill from there."

The chief gave a subtle nod.

"On Wednesday, neither of them showed up at the bar," Vikki said. "But they met at The Shack. We saw that on CCTV. Later Thursday night, the train driver calls in that he hit a car on the track around nine p.m."

"Mm-hmm, I remember that night," Levin said.

Vikki smiled. "I think that's what whoever put the body there wants us to believe, but Ted...Dr. Brandon, the new ME, says the driver was already dead before the train accident. Someone had fractured his skull before then killing him."

Levin leaned back. He took a deep breath and let it out through his nose. "This is the scenario I see. Mr. Bruno murders Mr. Darnel. He goes for a swim, and the long arm of karma grabs him, period." He cocked his head and shrugged. "We can work with that, yes? The public has nothing to fear. It involved two men with a score to settle. And they did a fine job taking care of business."

His eyes drifted from Gomez to Vikki. "Mattsen, you don't seem convinced."

Vikki raised her hands, then let them drop. "It could have happened that way, but it seems too easy."

"Most cases appear easy after they've been solved," Gomez said. "I think the captain is right." He smiled. "Hey, we should be thankful. A murder...two murders, solved with one stroke."

As Gomez spoke, Vikki crossed all the t's and dotted the i's. She had a nagging feeling they were missing something. But Gomez and the captain were ready to call it a day.

He turned to Vikki. "We're still waiting on toxicology. If everything is good, we wrap it up. If it doesn't, we start from square one."

"Fine with me," Levin said. "But I know it's already a slam dunk. See you later."

Vikki got up. That was a dismissal. She walked out of the office with Gomez right behind her.

Gomez said, "What next?"

Vikki sighed. "We should check out the rental vehicle."

Gomez raised his hand in surrender. "Sorry, Mattsen. We've solved the case already. You can tackle the car on your own for extra credit. I have some paperwork to take care of."

"No problem. I hope this ends soon. I have a ton to write myself."

"You better hurry. Rental companies are quick to write such vehicles off. Once CSU is done with it, it's taken to the junkyard and crushed."

"I better hurry up then," Vikki said.

CHAPTER TWENTY-THREE

The first policeman to arrive at the scene told Vikki where what remained of the car had been taken to.

At the junkyard on the outskirts of town, further down from Leisure Tavern, she was informed with regret that the vehicle had been crushed.

Her heart was squashed, but her spirit undaunted. Vikki headed to the accident scene. She might find something.

She passed a few farms with grazing cows, horses, and sheep munching on grass. The land stretched out in gentle undulating crests and valleys. She went by a solar farm, with panels covering a wide area absorbing the afternoon sun. The road and its surroundings were picturesque but isolated.

Vikki passed only two cars in the opposite direction in the ten minutes she'd turned off the main road. She stopped where the train track crossed the road. It was an unmanned crossing that had a single barrier. The killer had chosen an isolated spot.

She drove off the road and parked.

Vikki grabbed shoes covers, gloves, evidence bags from

the small stash she kept in her glove compartment. She covered her shoes and got out of the car. She looked around and noticed where the accident had occurred. It was a straight track after a bend. The train driver must have seen Darnel's car suddenly. Or maybe not at all.

There were dark oil stains and gouges in the ground, possibly made by the car as it was pushed forward by the train. Maybe it was a good thing Mark Darnel had already been dead before impact. It must have been terrifying being inside a car hit by a train.

Vikki took in the scene and imagined how it had played out. Till Bruno had driven up with Mark's dead body in the car; he must have been murdered somewhere else. Or they'd driven up together, and he'd killed him in the car.

Movies make killing someone appear easy. But apart from using a gun or if you're a trained killer, it's never an easy proposition. In equally matched individuals, especially in hand-to-hand combat, size, age, and physical condition come into play.

The element of surprise always skews the outcome of the fight to the person doing the surprise. Hit someone on the head hard with a baseball bat or something similar. You win the battle.

The individual with combat training fighting a non-trained individual is more likely to win. When it's two against one, the outcome is in favor of the majority. Did Till have an accomplice?

Vikki made a mental note to think of an alternative place where the murder had taken place, and for a murder weapon.

She continued her enacting in her mind. Till had driven the car with Mark's body onto the track. He'd got out and maneuvered the deadweight into the driver's side. Had he waited for impact, or had he left right away?

Vikki didn't have answers. She glanced around, hoping

there was CCTV somewhere. There was none. A cluster of bushes stuck out. If Till had hung around to ensure the deed was done, he must have hidden somewhere nearby.

She walked to the bushes. Something white hidden under some leaves caught her eyes. Heart pounding, she slipped on gloves and brushed the leaves. On the ground were three cigarette butts, sitting like truffles.

"Now, what do we have here?"

Two were crushed underfoot, but one was intact. Vikki's pulse raced. She took pictures of the ground and the butts with her phone. She brought out an evidence bag and scooped them up. She placed her hopes on the crime lab pulling some fingerprints or DNA from them.

Motivated, she traversed the area, hoping to hit pay dirt again. She found nothing else.

Vikki returned to her car, took off her shoe covers and gloves, and placed them in a bag. She drove back to the PD. She was eager to get the evidence to forensics.

As she drove along the long, windy road, a thought hit her. How did Till leave the accident scene? Did he walk-run? Was there a getaway car?

Her phone rang. She pulled it out from her back pants pocket. "Mattsen."

"Where are you?" It was Gomez.

"On my way back to the PD. I left the train accident scene a few minutes ago."

"I thought you went to the junkyard?"

"I did, but they'd crushed the car. So I went to the crash scene." She paused. "I found some cigarette butts. Before I forget, could you please pull Susan Beverly's financials?"

Gomez was quiet. "Why?"

"I have a hunch."

Gomez let out a breath. "And you don't want to share?

Anyway, we have a new development." Excitement was back in his voice.

"What is it?"

"It's above my pay grade. Come straight to the morgue. Ted will explain it better."

CHAPTER TWENTY-FOUR

Vikki didn't go straight to the morgue as Gomez had asked. First, she went to the forensic unit and dropped off the evidence bag.

"When do you want the result, Detective Mattsen?" the CSU tech asked.

"As soon as you can," Vikki said and rushed off.

At the morgue, she quickly pulled on protective clothing and went in. Gomez and Ted were in there already, all geared up.

Ted's eyes tracked her every move, a hint of a smile on his lips. Their eyes met. She smiled and looked away. Heat rushed through her. *Oh Lordy.* There was a palpable excitement in the air.

Gomez scowled. "It took you forever to get here."

"Good to see you, too," Vikki said. "I had to stop over at forensics. Remember I mentioned finding some cigarette butts? I went to drop them off. I feel the result from that will complement what you have here."

"Okay, Dr. Brandon. Please explain to Detective Mattsen what you told me?"

Ted smiled and placed a hand on his chest. "Sure." He turned to Vikki. "We were lucky. This is about Till Bruno—the drowning victim. The divers collected water samples around the watery grave when they retrieved the body. So I had the lab analyze the sample from the victim's lungs against that from the watery grave. They checked for the number of diatoms and the acidity of the water."

"What are diatoms?" Vikki asked.

Gomez smiled. "So we're in the same pay grade. I thought I was the only one with wood chips for a brain."

Dr. Brandon smiled. "It's no big deal. You had no reason to know about them. Anyway, they are tiny algae found in water. There's no doubt that the victim drowned, but the question is, where?"

Adrenaline surged through Vikki. Her heart raced. She swallowed. "What?"

Ted continued. "The water found in the lungs of our victim was different from that found in the lake. The water in his lungs was salty with low levels of diatoms. While the lake water has a higher concentration of diatoms and is not as salty."

"So he was killed somewhere else and dumped in the lake?" asked Vikki.

Ted nodded. "To be more specific, he drowned in clean water that had salt in it relative to the lake. So we're talking of something like a bathtub with bath salt. Also, he had in his system a high level of diazepam."

"Jesus," said Gomez. "So, he filled a hot tub with Epsom salt to soak his body and heal. Popped some benzos to help him relax. He fell asleep, slipped underwater, and drowned. Wasn't that what happened to Whitney Houston? She slipped underneath the water's surface in a drug stupor."

"Allegedly," Vikki said.

Dr. Brandon raised his hand. "Whether the OD, in this

case, was accidental or intentional, I can't tell. But one thing for sure is that the body was moved after death. He did not drown in the lake."

Gomez's eyes lit up. "Is it a coincidence that Mark Darnel and Till were moved after death?"

Vikki shook her head. "I don't believe in coincidences. Something is going on." She turned to Ted. "Thank you so much, Dr. Brandon."

"You know you can call me Ted, right?"

Heat rushed to Vikki's cheeks. "I know." She shifted her gaze to Gomez. "Did you get the financial report back for Susan Beverly?"

"It should be on my desk," Gomez said and headed for the door. "Let's go back upstairs and examine it." He waved at Dr. Brandon. "Thanks, Ted. Now I'm scared to get into a hot tub."

As they went upstairs, an image was forming in Vikki's mind, the picture getting clearer and clearer like a Polaroid picture. She had a hunch about what was in Susan Beverly's financial statement.

"Look at this," Gomez said, stabbing a finger at the piece of paper. Ms. Beverly had made a withdrawal of twenty-five thousand dollars from her account. The same day, twenty-five grand had showed up in Mark Darnel's account.

Vikki stood in front of the murder board. She'd printed a picture of Susan Beverly and pasted it on the board. Next, she put question marks under her image. She crossed out Maggie and Bruce. Then Till and Mark.

Gomez stared at the board. "You think Till killed Mark?"

"Likely," said Vikki. "But he had help. This is what I think. Mark Darnel comes out of jail in Florida. He finds out his boy Till is living large in New Jersey and sets out to meet him. He asks Till for money. Till doesn't have any, but his wife does. So he gets the money from her to pay Mark off."

Gomez shrugged. "Why didn't they go to the police?"

"Maybe they were being blackmailed. Anyway, they don't go to the police. They paid, and Mark came back for more. This time, Till says no."

"The killer or killers," Vikki said. "I think Mark Darnel was murdered somewhere else, put in the car, then driven onto the rail tracks. I hope the cigarette butts will help narrow down who we're looking for."

An investigator from CSU walked in and handed a sheet to Vikki.

"Thank you." She looked at it and smiled. "This sure helps." She handed the paper over to Gomez.

Gomez glanced at it and let out a whistle. "But the presence of the butt doesn't guarantee anything."

"True. But it places—"

Vikki was distracted by a commotion near the door. It was a familiar voice.

"I think you have the hots for me," said a woman with a Russian accent. "Why did you arrest me this time?"

It was the same tall blonde with a filthy mouth from yesterday talking to Maria Santiago. At least she wasn't drunk today.

Gomez cocked his head. "You think we should pay Ms. Beverly a visit?"

"About time," said Vickie. "About time."

CHAPTER TWENTY-FIVE

"Hi, Maggie, this is Detective Mattsen. I'm trying to drop off some personal effects for Ms. Beverly. Can I have her address, please?"

There was a pause, then Maggie said, "Sure, are you ready?"

Vikki wrote down the address. "One more thing, does Ms. Beverly own a boat?"

"A boat? No."

"Okay, no boat. That's it for now—thanks, Maggie." Vikki hung up.

Gomez drove. Susan Beverly's home was on the opposite side of the property where Vikki had met the older woman and her daughter the day the body had been discovered.

It was a modest one-story building, similar to the ones on the other side of the lake. It was one story high from the street, but behind opened to a two-story wall with glass panels for a commanding view of the lake.

"Do you think we'll get answers?" Gomez asked as they exited the police car.

"We'll find out soon," said Vikki and rang the bell. She gave it a few moments, then banged on the door.

Footsteps approached. The door swung open.

Susan stood there, in a white blouse and tan khaki pants, with light makeup. Her eyes widened. "Detective Mattsen—Detective Gomez. What a surprise." She made no move to invite them in.

"Can we come in?" Gomez said. "We have an update about Till Bruno."

Susan's eyebrows narrowed. "Update? What type of update?

"Sorry for not calling ahead. We're trying to close the case," Vikki said. "I think we're almost done. We'll only take a few minutes."

Susan raised an eyebrow. "Close the case? Come on in." She stepped aside.

Vikki entered to the faint odor of cigarette smoke in the air. Stress and loss had pushed Susan back to her low habits. In the living room was an open suitcase. "Are you going somewhere?"

"Yes. Sorry about the mess. Please sit." She pointed at a couch with a coffee table in front of it.

Vikki and Gomez sat. Pictures of Susan in the different roles she'd played over the years were on the walls. The home was furnished, like a second or vacation home.

Susan sat on the armrest of another couch. "We...we'd planned to go away before shooting started in my new role as the matriarch in this sitcom. Then Till...I'm sure he would have wanted me to go on my own."

"I'm sure," Vikki said. She quickly scanned her surroundings with darting eyes. She noticed the ashtray on the coffee table. "How long will you be away for?" It was filled with cigarette butts, Virginia Slims. The same brand she'd found by the railway track.

Susan followed her gaze. Then looked at Vikki. Their eyes met, and Susan glanced away, dipping her chin. "It's tough, especially right now. The chewing gums haven't done it for me yet."

"It's a journey," Vikki said.

Susan brushed a strand of hair behind her ear. "How can I help you close the case?"

"Yes, have you ever heard of Mark Darnel?" Vikki asked.

Susan thought for a second and shook her head slowly. "Is he a movie star?"

Gomez chuckled. "No, he and Till were old friends. In fact, we know he met with Till at Leisure Tavern. A bar on the outskirts of town."

"Till never mentioned him," Susan said, eyebrows furrowed.

"For some reason, we don't know yet," said Gomez, "he convinced Till to give him twenty-five thousand dollars. Do you know anything about that?"

The color drained from Susan's face. She fanned herself.

Like that day at her office, Vikki rushed to her. "Are you okay?"

"Can we step outside on the patio? I get these panic attacks when I think of Till." Susan stood up, walked to the patio door, and slid it open.

She walked through, and they followed.

Vikki shielded her eyes from the sun. Her gaze lingered on a sprawling white building on the other side of the lake. It was familiar. "Nice view. There was an accident on Thursday night, and Mr. Darnel's car was hit by a train."

Susan placed a hand on her chest. "My God. Hit by a train? Is he okay?"

Vikki raised her hand to her mouth to hide her surprise. Either Susan Beverly was an excellent actress, or they'd got it wrong. "You went to New York on Friday night, right?"

Susan nodded.

"Where were you on Thursday between eight and ten p.m.?" Vikki asked.

CHAPTER TWENTY-SIX

"I was right here with Till," Susan said. "That was the last sane day of my life. The next day...we argued. He left and never came home."

Gomez raised both hands. "Hold on. But are you sure you were home? Because we found cigarette butts similar to the one you have in the ashtray here close to the railway, where Mr. Darnel's car was hit by a train."

"And your fingerprint was found on the butt," Vikki said.

Susan's face looked like milk left in a glass overnight. "I-I wasn't there," she stammered. "I was home all night. I don't know any Mr. Darnel. You're both upsetting me. I'll have to ask you to leave now."

That was when Vikki remembered the picture in Susan's office. The background was a body of water and a white building. She pointed. "Is that Lake Front Restaurant?"

Susan, thrown off by the change in questions, glanced over her shoulder. "What—yes."

Vikki's pulse raced. The photo was taken right here. "Ms. Beverly, do you own a boat?"

Susan frowned. Her eyes drifted to her right, then back to Vikki. "Boat? No."

Vikki almost missed the panic that flashed through Susan's eyes. It quickly vanished. What was it that gave her such a concern? Vikki glanced in that direction. It was a hot tub hastily covered with a tarp with parts of it exposed.

Susan headed for the sliding door. "As I was saying, I have a plane to catch."

Vikki took a step toward the red hot tub. It had Marilyn Monroe written on the side in bold text, with that famous image of the star trying to hold down a blowing white halter dress while standing over a subway vent grill.

She remembered the hooker with a Russian accent at the police department Santiago had been trying to book, talking about getting her beauty sleep the day she'd been arrested. What had she said again?

I want to look like Marilyn Monroe when I wake up. Last night I saw her bobbing up and down on the lake.

Vikki was deep in thought. Could she have lifted the body all by herself? She must have done it in a clever way. "Is this what you used to get Till into the lake?" Vikki asked.

Susan froze, then continued toward the entrance to the house, her body shaking.

Gomez stepped forward and blocked her path to the door.

Vikki ripped off the cover from the tub. There was still water in it. She turned to Susan. "It's all over, Susan. The ME found enough sedatives to put an elephant to sleep in Till's system. You drugged him, drowned him, and dumped him in the lake."

Susan's legs gave out beneath her, and she dropped to her knees, crumpling into a heap. A cry escaped her lips. "No."

Gomez reached behind him and brought out cuffs. "Susan

Beverly, you are under arrest for the murder of Till Bruno. Interlock your fingers behind your head."

As she sobbed, he read her the rest of her Miranda rights and cuffed her.

"Why, Susan?" Vikki asked.

Tears flowed down Susan's face. "Oh God. Do-do you know what it feels like when people call you a washed-up actress? An old hag, behind your back?"

Vikki had no answer. But she'd felt helpless before.

"Or, we have no role for you. We want someone younger. Rejection after rejection—then I get a break. A role that I'm tailor-made for. And here comes Mark Darnel. He wanted twenty-five thousand dollars, or he'd tell everyone that my husband was an ex-con. I gave Till the money to pay him off. The next day I was planting new flowers when he showed up. He wanted another twenty-five thousand."

"Then what happened?" Vikki asked.

"I told him I didn't have it. And he said he'd bring me down. That new role, I was going to lose it. He'd make sure of that." Susan wailed. "No producer wants baggage with their actors. They'd drop me like a sack of potatoes once they heard my husband was an ex-con."

Gomez shook his head. "You should have come to us. You had options."

Vikki guessed what had happened next in Susan's head. Her brain had reacted to the psychological stress of Mark's threat as clear and physical danger—amygdala hijack. An immediate, overwhelming emotional response, triggered by the amygdala in the brain, bypassing rational thought processes.

"I panicked. I was so angry. I saw my dreams vanish before my eyes. I wasn't going to let it happen. As he turned to leave, I hit him on the head with a flowerpot. He fell and never got up."

Susan recounted the remainder of the story through tears and with a quavering voice, sounding like a child in third grade reporting a fight to a teacher.

Till had wanted to go to the police, but she'd said no.

"Having a murder case hanging over my head was a guaranteed way of getting axed from any show." They drove in two cars. The cigarette butts she'd dropped while they'd hidden behind a bush and waited for the train.

Till Bruno had still wanted to go to the police after, his conscience had got to him. She loved him, but sometimes you had to kill your darlings.

Susan had spiked his vodka with sedatives and got him in the hot tub. He went under within minutes. She'd put him in the lake with the help of Marilyn Monroe.

CHAPTER TWENTY-SEVEN

"So, you're saying that Ms. Beverly almost single-handedly carried all this out?" Angie asked.

Vikki sat at her desk in the squad room with Angie on the phone. The murder files on Till Bruno and Mark Darnel had been closed, and information was being gathered to prosecute Susan Beverly.

"Something like that," Vikki said, and she shoveled through some documents on her table. "Even though she confessed, we still had to gather information. The whole thing is sad. She didn't empty the hot tub. She only covered it with a tarp. The diatoms and chemical composition matched those recovered from Till's lungs."

"Well, it is what it is," Angie said. "I liked her. Anyway, I'm going to run with the story. It will be above the fold in print and on our website." There was a pause. "A little blue bird whispered in my ear that Dr. Edward Brandon will be running things as ME until further notice. I know you have *self*-imposed restrictions on where and who you date. This falls within the no-no area." Angie chuckled. "How are you going to navigate that?"

"Is all that—my personal life—going on your paper, too?" Vikki asked.

"Of course not," Angie said. "But, considering you'd already unwrapped the package twice and found it very satisfying, I imagine it might be hard to keep your paws away from it."

Vikki cocked her head and smiled sheepishly. She fanned herself with her hand. The best kept secrets are the ones you keep to yourself. Angie had her cornered. "It doesn't change anything. We are now coworkers, like Gomez and me." She knew she was lying to herself. "If we don't have more homicides back-to-back, our paths won't cross that much."

"Yeah, yeah, that's what they always say," Angie said.

Vikki knew deep down that was easier said than done. She must involve herself in some endeavor to keep her mind away from Ted. "Angie, I have to go."

"One more question. How did Susan get the body into the lake?"

"Her hot tub! It doubles as a boat. Who knew?"

"A boat that is a hot tub, too?" Angie asked.

"She did a commercial for a hot tub company years ago. They'd put a small outboard engine on one of their hot tubs and sailed it down a lake. Susan Beverly was one of the models in the tub. She acquired one after the shoot. She named it Marilyn Monroe."

"Wow, this is juicy. I'll have to amend my story."

Vikki continued. "She sailed out to the middle of the lake and tossed the body over. A hooker—"

"You mean escort," Angie said with a laugh.

"Okay, an escort mentioned she saw the boat in the lake, and that was how we made the connection."

"Thanks so much for that tidbit, Vikki. Now, duty calls. Have to go. See you later!"

"Talk soon." Vikki hung up.

The End.

ABOUT THE AUTHOR

Ifeanyi Esimai is a mystery and crime writer and enjoys reading across different genres. When he's not writing or reading, he's exploring documentaries on museums and ancient history.

Click here or the image to get all ten books!

Get a FREE copy of The Rookie!

Join my reader group for updates, giveaways, teasers, and a FREE copy of the prequel - The Rookie. Click here or scan the QR code

IFEANYI
ESIMAI
MURDER
IN
THE CIRCUS
VICTORIA MATTSEN CRIME SERIES

Prologue